Vaughan Williams

Copyright © 1997 Omnibus press
(A Division of Book Sales Limited)

Book edited byRoger and Elizabeth Buckley
Book typeset by Vitaset, Paddock Wood, Kent
Book Produced by Octave Books, Speldhurst, Kent
Cover Design and art direction by Studio Twenty, London
Cover photography by George Taylor

ISBN: 0.7119.6526.9
Order No: OP 47891

Exclusive Distributors:
Book Sales Limited,
8/9 Frith Street,
London W1V 5TZ, UK.

Music Sales Corporation,
257 Park Avenue South,
New York, NY 10010, USA.

Music Sales Pty Limited,
120 Rothschild Avenue,
Rosebury, NSW 2018, Australia.

To the Music Trade only:
Music Sales Limited,
8/9 Frith Street W1V 5TZ, UK.

Every effort has been made to trace the copyright holders of the photographs
in this book but one or two were unreachable. We would be grateful if the
photographers concerned would contact us.

Printed by Staples Printers Ltd, Rochester, Kent.

A catalogue record for this book is available from the British Library.

Visit Omnibus Press at http://www.musicsales.co.uk

Vaughan Williams

His Life and Times

by

Paul Holmes

Omnibus Press
London / New York / Sydney

Other titles in the series

Contents

Acknowledgements

By permission of Oxford University Press, I have included extracts and information from various publications including *Heirs and Rebels – Letters and Occasional Writings by Ralph Vaughan Williams and Gustav Holst* – edited by Ursula Vaughan Williams and Imogen Holst; *National Music and Other Essays* by Ralph Vaughan Williams, and *R.V.W. – a Biography of Ralph Vaughan Williams* by Ursula Vaughan Williams which provided valuable insights into the composer's later life.

A biographer is a magpie and a biography a magpie's nest. Some gems included may have been gathered, often unconsciously, over a lifetime's involvement with Vaughan Williams's music and I would like to apologise to any other source I may not have acknowledged. I would also like to thank Paul Elliott for his help and encouragement.

The publishers wish to express their profound gratitude to Ursula Vaughan Williams for her generous loan of photographs.

If any pictures remain unacknowledged we apologise and will be pleased to correct this in subsequent editions.

1 Early Years

Arthur Vaughan Williams.

Margaret Vaughan Williams.

'I don't know whether I like it, but it's what I meant', said Ralph Vaughan Williams about his Fourth Symphony. This modestly sums up the aims of a man whose search for a new voice in English music led him beyond narrow nationalism to experiment with many moods and styles. In doing this, he eventually achieved a synthesis that is unique and went on to create music that is loved and admired as much as any of his time.

For a man whose influence on twentieth century music was so great, it may seem strange that Vaughan Williams's roots lay very firmly in the Victorian era. English music at that time reflected an insularity based on the belief that art should somehow be subservient to imperial and commercial expansion or should simply provide a moral and religious basis for such activities. In these respects the confidence of Great Britain was unbounded. Its massive empire and world status fuelled the industrial might of its teeming cities, but beyond such 'dark, Satanic mills' stretched a deeply rural nation whose agricultural methods had simply been enhanced, not changed, by the Industrial Revolution. Although steam trains crossed the landscape at high speed, and farm machinery was also steam driven with ingenious inventions, all other forms of transport were horse-drawn. Village life continued much as it had since Saxon times with its close family units, its loyalties and notions of duty, its strict hierarchies of farm workers, middle class professionals and the gentry they looked up to. It was into a family of professional, landed squirearchy that Vaughan Williams was born on 12 October 1872 in the village of Down Ampney, Gloucestershire, where his father, Arthur Vaughan Williams, was the vicar.

Arthur Vaughan Williams came from a distinguished family of lawyers originally of Welsh extraction, but his wife, Margaret, had connections with the wealthy china-manufacturing Wedgwoods who owned a magnificent mansion, Leith Hill Place in Surrey. She also numbered Charles Darwin amongst her forebears. Ralph was their second son, although his elder brother Hervey and sister Meggie were close in age. Ralph was only two years old when his father died, leaving his mother to bring up her children virtually alone. She moved them to Leith Hill Place, where her father and sister Sophy still lived.

This fine country house was in many ways typical of hundreds of such houses of the period, with its many spacious rooms containing family portraits by Romney and Reynolds and other

The Vicarage, Down Ampney, where Hervey, Meggie and Ralph were born.

Ralph, aged about three years.

paintings by artists of the English school, including the almost obligatory animal studies by George Stubbs. Apart from this, the decor seems to have been austere, although there was a fine collection of Wedgwood pottery, yet the grounds surrounding it were filled with flowering shrubs and the views were magnificent, with the imposing Leith Hill and North Downs above and a panorama extending below through Surrey and Sussex to the South Downs above Brighton. Naturally, there were servants and nannies and, apart from being fatherless, the children lacked for nothing that people in their social position might have expected, although the atmosphere seems to have been more tolerant and less severe than in many other Victorian homes. In its cultured and liberal environment, private tuition began; the children read everything from fairy tales to Shakespeare, and music was naturally encouraged. Hervey learned the 'cello and Meggie the piano but it was Ralph who showed the greatest promise and who was given the greatest attention by his aunt. She taught him piano and some theory and the family bought an organ especially for him. He also made an attempt at composition with a piano piece called 'The Robin's Nest' at the age of six. Then, as he later wrote:

I remember as if it were yesterday, when I was about, I think, seven years old walking with my mother through the streets of Eastbourne and seeing in a music shop an advertisement for music lessons. My mother said to me, 'Would you like to learn the violin?' and I, without thinking, said 'Yes.' Accordingly, next day, a wizened old German called Cramer appeared on the scene and gave me my first violin lesson.

He progressed well on the violin which, as he later wrote, was his 'musical salvation' (he had found the piano difficult) and by the age of eight was capable of passing an advanced course

8

in harmony which Edinburgh University supervised by post.

This was clearly a happy time. There were holidays in Normandy and the family often stayed at Gunby Hall in Lincolnshire, or in Bournemouth where they had equally musical relatives. At home Ralph, his brother and sister enjoyed their sheltered existence and the usual children's pastimes. They had ponies and when the weather was bad entertained themselves with a toy theatre for which they wrote plays and for which Ralph composed and performed music. But formal education was inevitable and in 1883 Ralph was sent to school in Rottingdean, then a village near Brighton where the celebrated artist Sir Edward Burne-Jones lived and later the author Rudyard Kipling, but also a working farming and fishing community with a long folk song tradition that one hopes Vaughan Williams was not too protected to hear occasionally. Field House School (now St Aubyn's) is situated in the High Street and within sound of the sea and it is possible that snatches of folk singing might have drifted into the children's dormitories from the nearby pubs, where farm workers and fishermen relaxed amongst oil lamps and Sussex ales. He later revealed that he had his first official contact with folk songs at this time. He said of an edition of Christmas carols, 'my reaction to the tune of the Cherry-tree Carol … was more than simple admiration for a fine tune'; however the real discovery of raw English folk song would not come for Vaughan Williams until much later.

The school would not have encouraged fraternisation with the 'lower orders'. It was typical of many preparatory boarding schools designed for children of the upper middle classes before they attended public school proper. As such, it was organised in houses where the boys lived under the watchful eye of a house-

Field House.

master. Its syllabus laid a heavy emphasis on Greek and Latin, at which Vaughan Williams seemed to excel, and an even heavier emphasis on sport, at which he did not. He regarded cricket with indifference for the rest of his life. Although he joined in games, he enjoyed walking more. This was also to become a life-long passion and one easily encouraged by the proximity of the South Downs with their magnificent walks and panoramic views over Sussex to the hills above his home. Not that music was neglected, however, and Vaughan Williams continued to take lessons in violin and piano and began to discover the compositions of J.S. Bach. He persuaded his teachers to allow him to perform Raff's *Cavatina* at a school concert, and was permitted to attend a genuine orchestral concert in Brighton where he heard the music of Brahms conducted by the world-renowned Hans Richter.

Vaughan Williams left Field House in 1887 at the age of fifteen and entered Charterhouse, the public school where his brother had preceded him. It had originally been founded in 1611 but had moved from its London site in 1872 to the outskirts of Godalming, Surrey, not many miles from Vaughan Williams's home. Godalming is typical of many old country towns in the Surrey Weald, and the newly built but imposing Gothic structure of Charterhouse embodied many of its traditional English values, turning out its quota of professionals and empire-builders. Nevertheless, as in the best of such schools, the emphasis on *mens sana in corpore sano* was tempered with a flexibility that allowed a certain bending of the rules to accommodate gifted pupils. At this time Vaughan Williams was noted for his cheerful and pragmatic character and, although increasingly devoted to music, seems also to have done well academically. As usual, games were paramount, and Charterhouse at this time was at the vanguard of a resurgence of football.

Ralph at Charterhouse, middle of centre row.

As noted before, he was no great sportsman, despite growing into a strong if rather ungainly young man; however, he did enjoy playing tennis and croquet with his family.

Music was, according to Vaughan Williams 'mildly encouraged' at Charterhouse so he joined in all the musical activities available to him. He sang in the chapel choir, the repertoire being that of the Anglican Church – hymns and the unearthly beauty of services set by the Victorian English church composers, together with the occasional offering from Elizabethan times – Tallis or Orlando Gibbons. The school orchestra, in which he played second violin and later viola, catered for his more secular needs. Here, in addition to the more usual music of the classical masters, the then lesser-known *concerti grossi* of Corelli and Vivaldi were attempted.

11

In 1888, Ralph organised a concert at Charterhouse.

Vaughan Williams had moved on from his early efforts at composition and had begun to write songs and a little chamber music. He had continued to compose throughout his time at Field Place and to compose and play chamber music with family and friends during the school holidays, and so considered himself moving towards that most non-professional-class area, a musical career. With this in mind, he and a friend approached the headmaster of Charterhouse in August 1888 and requested the use of the school hall to put on a concert which would include a one-movement Piano Trio the young composer had written. 'Headmasters were headmasters in those days,' Vaughan Williams wrote, 'not the hail-fellow-well-met-young-feller-me-lads of modern times', but, perhaps amused by their presumption, he permitted it and attended it at the head of the whole school. Vaughan Williams did not actually play at what must have been the first public performance of any of his works, but, sandwiched between the fashionable Sir Arthur Sullivan and Louis Spohr, and sounding like derivative César Franck, his composition seems to have made a reasonable impression, even if stating it was left to the

Margaret Vaughan Williams (seated left) and Meggie (standing right) take a trip up the Nile with Lord and Lady Farrer and Godfrey Wedgwood (standing, left).

mathematics master who, as Vaughan Williams wrote: 'said in the sepulchral voice which Carthusians of my day knew so well, "Very good, Williams, you must go on." I treasured this as one of the few words of encouragement I ever received in my life.'

The remainder of his school days were unremarkable. He studied with the chapel organist, became a prefect, and before matriculating pressed his family to consider the possibility of a career in music. Even for an outwardly liberal family such as his, this was regarded as an unconventional step. The Army, the Law or the Church were considered more suitable professions for someone of his background, especially as he was a second son, and therefore not in line for a direct inheritance. The profession of musician was linked in the Victorian mind with that of the stage or some other such disreputable entertainment, and that of composer was far too insecure. There were notable exceptions of course: had not Mendelssohn been patronised by Queen Victoria herself? And then there were those fine, upstanding English composers whose morally uplifting hymns, oratorios and organ works were the staple of English musical life: Stainer, Goss, Parry, Stanford headed a diminishing list of mediocre tune-smiths. Of course the great Sir Arthur Sullivan had also made a success of satirical operetta, but who else was there to recommend in the moribund world of British music, a world so completely dominated by German models as to have no native spark at all? If Ralph had to follow such a path, a compromise would be permitted: he could study at the Royal College of Music in London with the view to becoming a church organist, and then he should follow in the family tradition and go to Trinity College, Cambridge to gain a more conventional university degree. This would allow him several options in due course.

So it was agreed, but first a short holiday was in order. In the summer of 1890, at the age of seventeen, Ralph left for Munich where he was to encounter the most powerful musical influence of the age.

2 The Young Musician

For any young Englishman wishing to become a composer at this time, Germany was an obvious place of pilgrimage. Without the blessing of its influence, there could be no pedigree to anything he composed. Even so, when he visited the country, Ralph Vaughan Williams knew very little of Beethoven and hardly anything of the living and, to English ears, very modern composer Brahms. It was not to these great classicists, however, that he owed his musical awakening, but to Richard Wagner who had then been dead for seven years. In between visiting the sights of Munich, and strolling round the art galleries and the English Garden, he attended a performance of *The Valkyrie* in the opera house where Wagner had conducted before his patron, Ludwig II of Bavaria. Such music was barely known in England, where it was still considered dangerously subversive, although the powerfully sustained crescendi and yearning chromaticisms of these heroic music-dramas had already seduced most of continental Europe, even in France where composers as different as Offenbach and Debussy were turning Paris into a mini-Bayreuth. Soon, many a young composer's emerging talent would be ship-wrecked on the rocks from which Wagner's Rhinemaidens sang. The naive young Vaughan Williams was in just such danger, for the effect on him was overwhelming but, as he wrote much later:

There was a feeling of recognition as of meeting an old friend which comes to us all in the face of great artistic experiences. I had the same experience when I first heard an English folk-song, when I first saw Michaelangelo's *Day and Night,* when I suddenly came upon Stonehenge, or had my first sight of New York City – the intuition that I had been there already.

With such impressions in his mind, Vaughan Williams returned to London to begin his studies in earnest.

Amidst the bustle of the largest city in the world, one might have been forgiven for not recognising its deep artistic philistinism. Through gratings in the middle of the streets, steam trains belched smoke from the world's first underground railway, testifying to the vision and ingenuity of the nation's engineers. It frightened the horses that still provided the only viable means of transport above ground. Although horses, horse-drawn omnibuses and hackney carriages still created work for crossing sweepers, the future, in the form of early cars or 'horseless

The City of London, early 1900s.

carriages' chugged past occasionally at 4 mph preceded by a man on foot with a red flag to alert pedestrians to their unpredictable and explosive danger. Despite this technological progress, vast areas of the city were still nothing more than the squalid slums Charles Dickens would have recognised. Their crooked streets frequented by prostitutes and terminating in gin palaces might all too suddenly be enfolded in choking smogs manufactured by hundreds of thousands of chimneys pouring coal smoke into the permanently filthy air.

Yet at the centre, where the wealth of its industrial and imperial might was focused, from the elegant, gaslit avenues with their smartly dressed people, their expensive stores and restaurants, past the theatres showing the latest melodrama or even a daring play by Pinero, to the monumental grandeur of its official architecture, London gave the impression of cultural hegemony. Only the patrons knew that not much more than an occasional revival of Shakespeare could be regarded as representing Englishness, and that entertainment rather than ideas was at the heart of English cultural life.

If ideas were the poor relations, music was in total poverty. Composers' models were Handelian oratorio and the Mendelssohnian equivalent that had been so much loved by Queen Victoria and Albert, her German consort. Even so, music was considered a trade for foreigners, mostly German or Italian, so that concert halls and the great Covent Garden Opera House in London provided little more. Music hall, romantic operas on fanciful themes, operettas in the style of Gilbert and Sullivan, military marches and church music were the staple fare of any Englishman who chose to compose. Anything more substantial was hardly

Sir George Grove.

considered worth a second look in a country the Germans had dubbed 'The Land Without Music'. The young Edward Elgar – whose name would eventually be the most famous in English musical circles – had attempted to make his name in London, but had been forced by grinding poverty to return to Malvern in the provincial Midlands the year before. At this time he was barely known beyond Worcester, where he had a few choral works performed at the Three Choirs Festival.

In such a desert, the Royal College of Music stood as an oasis of inspiration. Situated in a magnificent building next to the Royal Albert Hall, it was thus part of that educational complex created by Prince Albert which included the great museums of South Kensington whose exhibits ranged from modern science to fine arts. Although it had only been in existence for seven years, having been founded by the great musicologist Sir George Grove in 1883, it had gained an enviable reputation as a centre of excellence. Much of the credit for this must be handed to its director Dr Hubert Parry and its Professor of Composition, the Irishman Charles Villiers Stanford. These men were probably the most famous and influential serious composers in the country and, although both labouring heavily under German influence, had begun to encourage a spirit of genuine nationalism in music. Despite their standing, however, only their sacred music was given more than a polite hearing, their attempts at symphonies and operas never really bearing comparison with those of their foreign counterparts. It was to this world of musical provincialism that Vaughan Williams returned in the Autumn term of 1890 absolutely determined to compose.

He began by studying organ intensively with F.E. Gladstone, a cousin of the Liberal Prime Minister. This lasted for two terms, after which he had learned sufficient theory to enter Parry's composition class. Years later, Vaughan Williams talked about his experiences with him:

Parry and Stanford.

Many ... entirely misunderstood Parry; they were deceived by his rubicund bonhomie and imagined that he had the mind, as he had the appearance, of a country squire. The fact is that Parry had a highly nervous temperament. He was in early days a thinker with very advanced views. I remember, for example, how in the early nineties he accepted Ibsen with delight. He was one of the early champions of Wagner when other thinkers in the country were still calling him impious ...

In 1891 when I first went to Parry he was indeed an out-and-out radical both in art and life. He introduced me to Wagner and Brahms – which was quite contrary to curricula then obtaining in academies. He showed me the greatness of Bach and Beethoven as compared with Handel and Mendelssohn ...

Another unusual aspect of Parry was his wide-ranging intellect, and one particular area of his theories must have especially endeared him to Vaughan Williams, who was after all Charles Darwin's great-nephew:

Parry was a thinker on music, which he connected, not only with life, but with other aspects of philosophy and science. When Parry was a young man the Darwinian controversy was in full swing. He became a follower of Herbert Spencer and decided to find out how far music, as well as the rest of life, followed the laws of evolution. These thoughts he embodied in his great book, *The Evolution of the Art of Music*, in which he proves, conclusively to most people, that Beethoven's Ninth Symphony, for example, is not an isolated phenomenon, but a highly developed stage of a process of evolution which can be traced back to the primitive folk-songs of our people ...

Although Parry was not impressed with Vaughan Williams's composing talents, he corrected what Vaughan Williams modestly called 'my horrible little songs and anthems' with great attention. Vaughan Williams said his teacher, 'was always on the look-out for what was "characteristic" – even if he disliked the music he would praise it if he saw that it had character... Parry never tried to divorce art from life: he once said to me "Write choral music as befits an Englishman and a democrat." This attitude towards art led to an almost moral hated of mere luscious sound ...'

It was this hatred of sound for its sensual qualities alone that led Parry to detest most French music, especially opera. Nevertheless, Vaughan Williams managed to sneak off with a friend to see *Carmen* and also to hear Verdi when he had the chance. This was just as well, as he was sorely in need of as many chances to widen his knowledge of music as he could find. 'Parry could hardly believe I knew so little music', Vaughan Williams opined, and he was always grateful for his encouragement and advice, which ranged from playing him Beethoven sonatas, to suggesting which concerts he should attend, to lending him irreplaceable scores. He wrote: 'This was long before the days of miniature scores and gramophone records. I borrowed *Siegfried* and *Tristan* and Brahms's *Requiem*, and for some time after, my so-called compositions consisted entirely of variations of a passage near the beginning of that work.'

Although he did not lack money, Vaughan Williams enjoyed walking back to Leith Hill Place from the city (about 30 miles) as often as possible, and spent most of his spare time in the area around Dorking and the North Downs. Here, he still played chamber music with family friends and found the peace and comfort to compose. All passed agreeably enough until September 1892 when he entered Trinity College, Cambridge, to study history in addition to attending weekly lessons at the Royal College of Music. He also continued his music studies at Cambridge under the organist and composer Charles Wood with a view to taking his B. Mus. degree. Vaughan Williams considered Wood 'the finest technical instructor I have ever known'. Such an arrangement was not as unusual as it would appear, for the Royal College of Music maintained close links with Cambridge, where Stanford was also Professor of Music, and the frequent rail service between the capital and the ancient university town meant Vaughan Williams could travel between them with hardly any strain on his curriculum.

It also meant that he could attend musical events in London, and one such opportunity had occurred early in 1892 when he visited The Royal Opera House at Covent Garden to hear Gustav Mahler conduct a heavily cut version of Wagner's *Ring* cycle over four evenings. He also conducted *Tristan and Isolde*, which so moved and excited Vaughan Williams that he could not sleep that night. Unknown to him, another young man in the audience with composing ambitions was also undergoing an almost religious conversion during this feast of Wagner – a young man who was eventually to have more influence on him than the master of Bayreuth and was to become his most valued friend and trusted collaborator when they finally met – Gustav Holst.

At Cambridge, Vaughan Williams entered into the musical spirit of what was possibly the most cosmopolitan establishment in England. He made friends with the brilliant organ scholar Hugh Allen and joined the University Music Club, which, as its name suggests, was more informal than the staid University Music Society. The Club was concerned with chamber music and its concerts would often include lampoons, satires and comic songs in which both academics and undergraduates would take their turns to amuse the company. The Society concerts, on the other hand, were mostly given over to large orchestral and choral works, and there were chapel choirs and organ recitals which Vaughan Williams regularly attended in addition to the obligatory church services on Sundays. He also found time to conduct a choral society, where he introduced some rarely performed Schubert masses and pursued a new-found interest in the music of Weelkes, Morley, Tallis and Byrd.

Occasionally, he walked across the Cambridgeshire fens as far as the awe-inspiring bulk of Ely Cathedral which rose eerily out

18

of the levels, and heard the services sung inside. Those who have never attended such services, especially that of Evensong, cannot completely understand their sheer aesthetic and emotional appeal. This can be appreciated even by those who are not particularly religious. It is an experience which is at the heart of Englishness, and it is one that began a lifelong love and fascination in the young Vaughan Williams despite the fact that he was by now veering sharply towards atheism.

Vaughan Williams was fortunate in having a well-connected cousin studying at Cambridge at the same time as himself. Ralph Wedgwood introduced him to a group of brilliant young men, most of whom went on to make an important mark in the world. These included G.E. Moore, the philosopher, and George Trevelyan, the historian. He also met Bertrand Russell who interested him in the poetry of the American, Walt Whitman, then enjoying a vogue in England. Undergraduate Cambridge provided enviable privileges and pleasant social entertainments and Vaughan Williams joined in as many as he had time for. He began to dress flamboyantly and went punting on the river Cam. He attended dances, and sampled the new vogue for cycling on pneumatic tyres through the flat Cambridgeshire landscape. In the holidays, he spent weeks with his new friends in 'Reading Parties' at a cottage in Seatoller, Borrowdale – considered one of the most beautiful valleys in the Lake District – where walking and cycling were the only interruptions to long sessions of reading and discussion.

It was in Cambridge that he was reacquainted with a child-hood friend – Adeline Fisher, a member of an artistic and well-connected family. Adeline occasionally came to stay with her sister, who had married one of the dons, although Ralph had not seen her since their two families had known one another many

Seatoller House.

19

Adeline Fisher in 1896.

years before, and he soon noticed that she had grown into an intelligent and beautiful young woman who was also an accomplished performer on 'cello and piano. Soon there was a small chamber group formed with Ralph, Adeline and two other friends, Ivor and Nicholas Gatty, which met whenever she was in Cambridge and eventually Ralph's feelings for her began to develop beyond those of a shared interest in music and intelligent conversation. He was delighted to find that these feelings were reciprocated.

Vaughan Williams obtained his B. Mus. in 1894 and went on to gain a Second in History the following year. But he was still not satisfied. His music tutors regarded him as little more than a dilettante composer with no promise of significance, although they thought he might eventually be an adequate performer. His main official instrument was still the organ and he decided that he would best be able to continue composition studies in tandem with this more practical skill, so he returned full-time to the Royal College of Music in London where he entered the class of its most distinguished organ teacher, Sir Walter Parratt, and obtained a job as organist and choirmaster at St Barnabas's, a church in South Lambeth, taking lodgings nearby. Although this was an unpromising post in a meagre part of London, and one he was to heartily detest in time, later confiding that being an organist was 'a trade for which I was entirely unsuited', he found the experience useful, writing subsequently: 'I founded a choral society and an orchestral society, both of them pretty bad, but we managed once to do a Bach Cantata and I obtained some of that practical knowledge of music which is so essential to a composer's make-up.'

He had also shown his family that he could find gainful employment in the world of music and felt justified in enrolling for Stanford's composition class at the College.

Vaughan Williams had found his organ, as opposed to piano, studies relatively painless, but he soon discovered that Stanford could be a hard taskmaster. He was often cold, overbearing and aloof, although his fellow-Irishman Bernard Shaw, then a music critic of great influence in London, thought his music was 'eccentric, violent, romantic, patriotic'. He was heavily influenced by Brahms, but could still write original as well as recognisably Irish music, most especially in such overtly nationalistic works as his Third Symphony and Irish Rhapsodies. Despite his manner, he had an almost freakish sense of humour, as on the occasion when he set a series of limericks by Edward Lear and others to music parodying the 'greats': Wagner, Beethoven, Brahms, et al., and claimed they were the work of one Alexander Drofnatski – Stanford backwards! The bluff and at times dismissive attitude for which Stanford was famous hid a shrewd and intuitive mind, and most of his pupils grew to value such remarks as, 'your music is all Brahms and water, me bhoy, and more water than Brahms!' or 'it won't do, me bhoy, it won't do' as more helpful than scornful.

Vaughan Williams, however, was in no mood to be patronised.

He was a working post-graduate and later remarked on his return to full-time studies, '… by the time I became a pupil of Stanford's I was musically more mature and did not fall under his spell as completely as I did under that of Parry.' As a result, Vaughan Williams was perhaps more critical of his methods than less mature students might have been and less liable to put up with his brusque vagaries. He later acknowledged his debt to and his affection for the man, but had no illusions about him nonetheless, as he shows in this reminiscence:

He was a true Irishman, quarrelsome and at the same time loveable and generous. Though artistically we were poles apart, I had for him that affection which certain types of man seem to call up. He was intolerant and narrow-minded and it was this, I think, which made him a good teacher … Stanford was often cruel in his judgements and the more sensitive among his pupils wilted under his methods and found comfort under a more soft-hearted teacher. I remember I once showed Stanford the slow movement of a string quartet. I had worked feverishly at it, and, like every other young composer, thought not only that it was the finest piece that had ever been written, and that my teacher would fall on his knees and embrace me, but that it was also my swan song. Now what would Parry have done in a case like this? He would have pored over it for a long time in hopes of finding something characteristic and, even if he disliked the piece as a whole, would try to find some point to praise. Stanford dismissed it with a curt 'All rot, me bhoy!' This was cruel but salutary. So far as I can remember, he was quite right. Luckily the piece was lost years ago …

… When I was Stanford's pupil I made the great mistake of fighting my teacher. A great deal of our meagre lesson time was occupied with the discussion of whether one of my progressions was damnably ugly or not, which time might have more profitably been spent on the larger issues. Anything crude or clumsy, – or 'ugly', as he called it – was anathema to Stanford …

However, Vaughan Williams concludes with praise for his teacher: 'With Stanford I felt I was in the presence of a lovable, powerful and enthralling mind; this helped me more than any amount of technical instruction.'

Vaughan Williams found more useful support amongst his contemporaries. He had fallen in with the Kensington Tea Shop Set – a student-composer group which met in this setting and discussed 'every subject under the sun from the lowest note of the double bassoon to the philosophy of *Jude the Obscure*' as they sampled their tea and crumpets. Vaughan Williams later wrote: 'I learnt more from these conversations than from any amount of formal teaching, but I felt at a certain disadvantage with these companions: they were all so competent and I felt such an amateur.'

These young men included Gustav Holst, John Ireland, Fritz Hart, Thomas Dunhill and Samuel Coleridge-Taylor, but it was Gustav Holst who was to become his closest friend during the two years Vaughan Williams was to stay at the Royal College of Music.

On the face of it they seemed unlikely kindred spirits. Although both came originally from Gloucestershire and both were addicted to long-distance walks and cycling, their circumstances were very different. Vaughan Williams was a Cambridge graduate coming from a rich, well-connected Establishment family and with no money problems of his own, but Holst was the son of a hard-working Cheltenham musician originally of German and Scandinavian stock. He had had a financial struggle to study composition at all and had subsisted on an income of £1 a week since his arrival at the Royal College of Music in 1892. Even by late nineteenth century standards this was a meagre amount. Although eventually granted a scholarship, he had to supplement this by playing the trombone in dance halls and seaside bands. The two men were physically oddly-matched as well. Vaughan Williams was large and sturdy with the look of an untrained athlete, sometimes expensively over-dressed with the air of the Aesthete made so fashionable by the Café Royale set. Holst was shorter, thin and pale, dressed shabbily, and suffering from short-sight and a neuritis in his right arm which had curtailed his chances of becoming a concert pianist – although he could still play the organ and trombone – and made the ordinary business of writing down his compositions at times almost unbearable. Yet kindred spirits they were, and were to remain so until Holst's death forty years later.

The most important part of their collaboration began immediately. They decided to criticise each other's compositions mercilessly but honestly and to set up what they termed 'field days' at each other's lodgings to work through any improvements they might mutually suggest. 'What one really learns from a college is not so much from one's official teachers as from one's fellow-students,' Vaughan Williams wrote later, and it is clear that these field days proved invaluable to them both as each struggled to find an individual and essentially English musical voice. They also joined the college's Literary Society. Apart from the interest in Pre-Raphaelite literature, Swinburne, novels and poems by George Meredith and Thomas Hardy which was usual at that time, they also read widely in European literature. A.E. Housman became another influence when he published his sequence of poems *A Shropshire Lad* in 1896. This work bowled over the younger generation and was to become seminal for poets and composers alike, possibly the text by a contemporary English writer which was most often set to music in the earlier years of the new century. The Debating Society also heard them speaking on such issues as 'The Future of English Music', advocating the abolition of academic training, and they struck a blow against the bourgeoisie by proposing that 'The Moderate Man is Contemptible'.

It was a heady time for debate with radical ideas in the air and Holst interested Vaughan Williams in the idealistic Fabian-style Socialism of William Morris and Bernard Shaw. Morris's writings in particular had come to fruition in his own Arts and Crafts

22

An early letter from Vaughan Williams to Holst.

movement with its ideals of Medieval craftsmanship flying in the teeth of Victorian mass production, but it was the egalitarian ideas he preached that inspired them both, Holst even going so far as to join the Hammersmith Socialist Society which met at Morris's house, making himself useful by conducting their choir in daring works such as Elizabethan madrigals, Purcell and Wagner. Although not being so committed as to join with his friend, Vaughan Williams warmed to such ideas. His radical and Liberal background made him a natural sceptic and he was always ready to question the establishment, especially when he was in the less

23

responsible role of student. Despite being involved with church services and having a deep and abiding love of Anglican church music, his views were still strongly tinged with radical atheism although they would eventually settle into a quizzical agnosticism, suspicious of all extremes.

By 1897 Vaughan Williams decided that he had learned as much as he could profitably use at the Royal College of Music and that he must move on. He had been engaged to Adeline Fisher for nearly three years now, and the two decided to marry in October of that year. There was no opposition from either family as they seemed ideally matched both in background and tastes, so it was arranged. One irksome duty had to be relinquished first, however: his post at St Barnabas's.

Vaughan Williams was certainly no snob and could have been reasonably content in a post that at least placated his family with the status of a steady musician's job: he found it rewarded his efforts, but he was constantly frustrated. In a letter to Holst in the summer vacation he bemoaned the laxity of the people he had to deal with, asking him to stand in for him:

… I am leaving this damned place in October and going abroad. Suppose you were offered it would you consider the matter? The screw is £50 and the minimum duties:
   Monday: boys any time after 6.0
   Wed: boys 7.0 service 8.0-9.0
   Thurs: full practice 8.30 or 8.15 till 10 or past if you can get them to stop.
   Sunday: 11.0 with choral communion once a month 7.0 and children's service at 3.0 once a month.
   Besides this you are supposed to run the choral society whenever it intermittently exists, and give occasional organ recitals.

Holst was at that time 'Worming' as he called it: working the season with his seaside bands in Brighton and Blackpool under the direction of the endearingly named Stanislaus Wurm, but he showed interest. Vaughan Williams wrote back to him giving him further details of the job but indicating his disgust for it in no uncertain terms:

… those louts of men will slope in about 8.45 and make you mad – the only ones who can sing will be away; let the boys go by 9.30. If you like you can keep the louts on but there is no necessity …

After their marriage in All Saint's Church, Hove, Sussex on 9th October, Ralph and Adeline took an extended honeymoon abroad, but it was, by mutual consent, a working honeymoon. It began in Berlin where an uncut performance of *The Ring* was being given. The couple had anticipated this by playing the entire piano score through together before setting out. They stayed until December, and heard *The Ring* and much else. Vaughan Williams recalled:

Ralph photographed by Adeline near Bolzano in Italy, 1897.

I heard all the music I could when I was in Berlin, especially operas. Among them were Lortzing's *Undine* and Meyerbeer's *Robert Le Diable*. I also remember beautiful performances of Bach Cantatas at the Sing-Akademie. The Joachim and Halir quartets were at their zenith and there was a memorable performance at the Hochschule of the Brahms Double Concerto played as a pianoforte trio by Joachim, Hausman, and Barth.

They also visited the sights of the capital, impressed by the churches, museums and palaces as well as the monuments rising to the recent imperial ambitions of the newly created German Empire. Prussian militarism and cultural excess seemed to lie uneasily side by side but their enthusiasm for Berlin was undimmed. Vaughan Williams was there to further his musical education and enrolled at the *Hochschule Für Musik*, where he took lessons from Max Bruch.

Bruch was a classicist in the Brahmsian mould, a good second to the great Brahms himself, who had died six months earlier in Vienna. Bruch was reported to be a man so difficult to deal with that at least one orchestra had petitioned to have him removed as their director, yet he and the young Englishman seemed to get on well together. Bruch was mildly interested in folk songs, as both Brahms and Beethoven had been in their own limited way, and Bruch's *Scottish Fantasy* is still performed as a successful testament to his use of folk colour in orchestral dress. Yet this was not a profound interest so much as a reworking of tuneful themes at an appropriate moment – a patronising glance from 'High Art' down on 'peasants merrymaking'. Even such 'composers of the people' as the Czech Dvořák had used folk songs simply to enhance the recognised classical structures that had not changed since Haydn's time, and Vaughan Williams learned little in this area from Bruch or the other continental composers of the generation, although he remembered: 'I worked hard and enthusiastically … and Max Bruch encouraged me, and I had never had much encouragement before.'

Continuing south through Italy, Ralph and Adeline arrived in San Remo, where they spent Christmas. They returned to Berlin for a short period before visiting Prague – then, as now, one of the finest medieval cities in Europe, and Dresden – then, but unfortunately not now, possibly the finest baroque city in the world. Both these places had exceptional musical associations – Prague as the vibrant centre of a nationalistic school of composers who were using Czech folk music as a means of establishing an independent political identity within the dying Austro-Hungarian Empire, and Dresden as a centre of German music descending from the eighteenth century in an unbroken line.

In 1898 Ralph and Adeline returned to London and set up home in a series of temporary furnished rooms, ending up in Cowley Street, Westminster. Vaughan Williams recalled: 'I settled down to try and learn how to compose, not by studying but by doing,' but he also worked hard for his diploma as a Fellow of the

Ralph (viola) and Adeline ('cello), with their friends René and Nicholas Gatty, about 1900.

Royal College of Organists and on a thesis for his doctorate. It was fortunate that he had a private income, for such single-minded exertions took up most of his day.

The couple began to draw a circle of close friends around them including the 'Tea Shop Set' from the Royal College of Music, friends from Ralph's 'Magic Circle' at Cambridge and relatives on both sides. There was much amateur music-making, most often with a group of friends who banded themselves together in a string quartet affectionately nick-named 'The Cowley Street Wobblers'. Here Vaughan Williams would contribute the viola part. Holst was still studying at the Royal College of Music, and still 'Worming' although he also had found the St Barnabas appointment intolerable and had not continued there long, passing the post on to his fellow-student, John Ireland. Together, Ralph and Gustav pursued their mutual criticism and worked on specific 'field days' to improve their music.

Vaughan Williams was now producing chamber music, part-songs and other choral works in the English ecclesiastical tradition, plus songs to texts by Tennyson and the Pre-Raphaelites, who still exercised a powerful aesthetic and cultural influence over the period. The *House of Life* song cycle which he wrote several years afterwards set words by Rossetti, whilst the song *Linden Lea* belongs to this early period and is the first of his songs to be still regularly sung as well as remaining one of his most popular. The text was originally written in Dorset dialect by William Barnes, a friend of the novelist Thomas Hardy, and in his setting of it the composer seems to be moving towards a recognisable voice of his own, despite still being in thrall to Germanic models in more ambitious projects.

By 1899, when Vaughan Williams gained his Doctorate in

Music from Cambridge, it seemed that there was nothing more he could learn academically, yet he was still painfully unsure of his direction. He knew that it lay somewhere in the traditions of English Church music which he admired more deeply than ever, but he realised that, as a rational thinker and nominal unbeliever, his total commitment could not rest there. He was as completely aware as any English musician of the glories of Purcell and of his predecessors, yet also knew that there had been nothing comparable since Purcell's death two hundred years before. He admired Wagner, but sensed the stranglehold such music could have on his English roots. He had the example of the emerging political nationalism of Europe's suppressed minorities who saw a window into their true identity through indigenous folk music, yet he could not transfer their fire to any sense of resentment at English political suppression. The suppression of English identity was occurring culturally from within, and he began to sense that he must look deeper into its native traditions if he were to synthesise a truly national voice.

3 A New Direction

If those seeking an English cultural identity lacked the anger and fervour of their European counterparts, they did not lack well-meaning enthusiasm. Different individuals had collected ballads and folk songs at various times throughout the nineteenth century, and John Gay's eighteenth-century *Beggar's Opera* had been almost exclusively based on contemporary ballads. There was, however, a lack of focus in these individuals' efforts and the few national songs that had been published had been largely sentimentalised out of recognition for use in Victorian drawing rooms. Some enthusiasts, including those such as Parry and Stanford who were attempting to find a way into an English musical renaissance, knew that a rich store of indigenous music lay as much with the ordinary people of England as it did with those of Wales, Scotland and Ireland. Collections had been published in the 1890s and the names of Baring-Gould, Lucy Broadwood and Fuller Maitland are prominent in the area, but it was not until 1898 when the Folk Song Society was founded that there was any real attempt to co-ordinate a nation-wide search.

The problem was that these well-meaning people were largely urban academics and the search relied on second-hand information filtering through to their dusty middle-class studies. They also seemed to be unaware of the real nature of folk song or of the circumstances in which it was still regularly performed. Few can ever have set foot in a country pub where real farm workers gathered after desperately hard physical labour and relaxed with these songs. The academics also discovered their texts were often earthy, and had to be toned down for polite use amongst the heavy furniture and antimacassars, whilst their single vocal line had to be harmonised for drawing room pianos. Often it turned out that what were sometimes regarded as folk songs were actually carefully crafted ballads written by Grub Street hacks for the urban proletariat in response to some distant topical event. The upshot of this was that the search produced little as it progressed, and what it did produce was a stilted approximation of the songs' original vitality.

One man stood out from all the rest, however – Cecil Sharp. Although he might have been considered an academic – he was Principal of the Hampstead Conservatory in London – he was not originally associated with the Folk Song Society but had become interested in folk song independently as he researched the area for material for his students to sing. By 1899 he had grown impatient with the methods of his musical colleagues, and decided to travel amongst the people to discover the real flavour of their music. In doing this he was using the methods his contemporaries used in Europe in the fast-disappearing peasant communities of Hungary, where Bartŏk and Kodaly were beginning to record Transylvanian songs and dances on Bell's recently patented cylinder recording machine. Sharp toured the English West Country and began to publish his findings. Over the following five years he broadened his field, and his discoveries were a revelation to those who had thought the activity a worthy but basically peripheral area of research. Vaughan Williams was aware of Sharp's activities and eventually met him in 1900, but his own interest was still slow to develop, as his technique was not yet ready for such an influence.

Vaughan Williams had been conscious of a personal affinity with English folk music since his childhood and later described how, as early as 1893, he had encountered a version of the tune *Dives and Lazarus* and had 'that sense of recognition – "here's something which I have known all my life, only I didn't know it!".' Part of Vaughan Williams's original blindness to the potential of folk song may have been his inability at that time to see how he might absorb it into a serious symphonic style. There were many precedents, of course: Dvořák and Smetana in Bohemia, and the Russian nationalists, had all used folk music in their symphonic structures, yet there was some truth in the opinion that their themes could not be developed satisfactorily, and that, in the old jibe, the only thing a composer could do once he had played a folk song was to play it again – louder! Many composers had produced pleasing work in the form of orchestral suites that did little more than arrange a series of songs and dances, but Vaughan Williams and his constant gadfly Holst were after more substantial prey and were not at that time ready to pursue folk song up what was still considered a blind alley. And there was the example of Edward Elgar, the latest modern English composer of any substance to receive enthusiastic applause when his *Enigma Variations* were first performed in London in June 1899, a performance that both Vaughan Williams and Holst had attended. This seemed to prove that the new forward trend in English music was still firmly rooted in the German symphonic tradition. Other composers were attempting to marry folk song and the Germanic tradition to their own personal styles but some, like Frederick Delius, found England too stifling for them. English Philistinism and his own uncompromising atheism had driven him abroad, and his music, although it would become an important strand in the new English musical revival, was virtually unknown at this time.

It was in 1899 that Ralph and Adeline moved into their first permanent home, taking a lease on 10 Barton Street, a substantial house in Westminster. Although its plumbing was rudimentary the house provided a measure of privacy: they could entertain their friends and relatives, it had a small work-room for Ralph, and he could keep a cat – the first of many of those endearing creatures with whom he felt a great affinity. The couple were to live there for another six years. These were quietly domestic rather than outwardly eventful, the comfortable round of middle-class existence moving calmly from year to year broken by the occasional holiday with relatives in Yorkshire or the West Country, although Adeline was eventually pre-occupied by her brother's nervous illness caused after serving in the Boer War and would occasionally spend weeks in Hove nursing him. Ralph began to write articles for the *Vocalist*, a musical magazine, contributing thoughts on such topics as Beethoven and Bach, Wagner and what exactly constituted an 'English' school of music. He also taught music part-time at a girls' school and gave the equivalent of Adult Education lectures at London University and in the suburbs and surrounding districts of the capital. He still managed to spend a least eight hours a day composing, although, as he recalled:

I still felt the need of instruction, and in about the year 1900 I took my courage in both hands and wrote to Elgar asking him to give me lessons, especially in orchestration. I received a polite reply from Lady Elgar saying that Sir Edward was too busy ... But though Elgar could not teach me personally he could not help teaching me through his music. I spent several hours at the British Museum studying the full scores of the *Enigma Variations* and *Gerontius*.

With these studies fresh in his mind, his orchestration became more polished, although it was still heavily Teutonic. He wrote to Holst, who had finished his studies and was then touring as *répétiteur* with the Carl Rosa Opera Company: 'Did I tell you that I was setting "The Garden of Proserpine" to music for chorus & orchestra with lots of trombones and things – I've just finished the first sketch – a sort of 6 lined affair most of it ...'

He continued to write music in this vein as well as doing a certain amount of editing, including an edition of Purcell's *Welcome Odes* for the Purcell Society. Writing again to Holst, he reported: '... I've finished my "Bucolic Suite" and written a song and made a rough copy of the Trombone thing and finished a volume of Purcell and am starting another thing called a "Sentimental Romance"...'

A few of these early orchestral works were performed over the next few years in the Winter Gardens, Bournemouth by a champion of young English composers, Dan Godfrey. These pieces added Vaughan Williams's name, together with Holst's, to the list of emerging young talent gaining the public's attention, but they show little individuality and were, together with two quintets and much else from the period, eventually disowned by the composer. They do, however, reveal a firm grasp of technique and a tentative experimentation, at what was a time of great change both for himself and the surrounding world.

In 1901 Queen Victoria died, and, as the crowds watched the great imperial procession following her coffin through the streets of London, many realised that a whole era had effectively come to an end. In some senses, the 'Victorian' period had already ended: the twentieth century, although still clothed in top hats, frock coats and voluminous dresses, buzzed with a new excitement. Electric light was beginning to replace gas and oil, horseless carriages, now permitted to travel freely, were more common on the streets whilst the first high-performance car had been tested by the German manufacturer Benz. Telephones and relay cable carried information at unheard-of speeds and Marconi had made his first Morse code broadcast across the Atlantic. The biograph picture houses showed moving images to the masses – even the funeral of the great Queen-Empress herself could be viewed in their comfortable darkness for a few pennies – and a feeling of optimism greeted the accession of her son, inaugurating the new Edwardian Age.

But such a ferment of technological change had its disadvantages. Rural communities were fast disappearing, already unsettled by a hundred years of urban industrialism and the social unrest which mechanisation had caused amongst time-honoured customs. As the suburbs of the wealthier middle classes expanded outwards from the great cities, rural identities were being erased. If rearguard actions were being fought by such thinkers as William Morris and such archivists as Cecil Sharp, they seemed to grow weaker as the new century began to gather momentum. Soon, it seemed, it would be too late to capture the soul of the nation as it was perceived by such men.

Gradually, Vaughan Williams was drawn into their concern. He longed to find that elusive national character in music, and wrote in the *Vocalist* in 1902:

What we want in England is *real* music, even if it be only a music-hall song. Provided it possesses real feeling and real life, it will be worth all the off-scourings of the classics in the world ...

But he was not ready to recognise the possibility of any emerging enthusiasm for folk music being 'a universal remedy' for native English composers, and his articles expressed his doubts at the time. He was aware that folk songs came from a peasant class that virtually no longer existed and in which English composers had never had any roots. Grafting such songs on to their style would only produce artificial fruit. 'In former times,' he wrote, 'musical England came to grief by trying to be foreign; no less surely shall we now fail through trying to be English', and he concluded, 'the national English style must be modelled on the personal style of English musicians.' His struggle over the following years would be to achieve that personal style. At this time his compositions included a song cycle setting R.L. Stevenson's *Songs of Travel*. This, like Housman's *Shropshire Lad*, represented an idealised version of rural life. Stevenson's vagabond celebrates open fires and the romance of the open road but, despite Vaughan Williams's fresh tunefulness the songs still lacked much sense of contact with the soil of England.

Another main concern of his was the low status of music in England, where there were few truly professional orchestras, one of the exceptions being the Queen's Hall Orchestra in London under Henry Wood, who had inaugurated his successful series of Promenade Concerts there in 1895. The Coronation of Edward VII in 1902 had also given him little reason for encouragement, producing the usual 'official' music, the most memorable probably being Elgar's *Coronation Ode* expanded from his first 'Pomp and Circumstance' march and containing the immortal nationalist anthem 'Land of Hope and Glory'. It was clear that Elgar was destined to become the most honoured English composer of the new decade and the 'imperial' style he used for such occasions the one most readily acceptable to English ears. Vaughan Williams's isolation as a composer preyed on him, as it did on Holst who suggested his own remedy in a letter he sent to Vaughan Williams from Berlin where he was honeymooning in 1903:

Seeing foreigners is a mistake as a rule. Don't you think we ought to victimize Elgar? Write to him first and then bicycle to Worcester and see him *a lot?* I wish we could do that together. Or else make a list of musicians in London whom we think worthy of the honour of being bothered by us and *who have time and inclination to be bothered* and then bother them ... It would be dreadful while it lasted but I think the effect would be good.

Somehow we seem too comfortable – we don't seem to strain every nerve. Anyhow I know I don't. And composing is a fairly impossible affair as things go even at the best of times ... As for conducting (which we ought to learn) it is impossible to attain in England and I fear we must give up all hopes of it. As an orchestral player I really do feel sorry, as England is crying out (unconsciously) for real conductors. Henry J. [Wood] is the nearest approach ... *And it is not all a question of unlimited rehearsals* ...

It was probably the folk song enthusiast Lucy Broadwood who first made Vaughan Williams aware that the genre was worth preserving and that there was little time in which to do it. After his meeting with her in 1902, he became seriously concerned that a national cultural asset was dying with the last folk singers and he began to give lectures on it to his Adult Education classes. By December 1903, he had travelled as far as Brentwood in what was then rural Essex, and so fired his audience of middle-aged matrons with enthusiasm that they asked him to a vicarage tea party in Ingrave close by, where they intended to encourage some of the villagers to perform their old songs.

The whole idea must have seemed hopeless. Never could the class divisions that Vaughan Williams loathed so much in English society have seemed so evident as at this well-meaning event. On his arrival, he found his hosts busily dispensing tea to the scrubbed and starched villagers sitting uneasily in the parlour dressed in their Sunday best, but when the politenesses were concluded and the guests asked to perform, none was forthcoming. One may imagine the strain. However, Vaughan Williams knew how to talk directly with people of all classes without patronising them – a knack he had learned in childhood at Leith Hill Place where, radically for the time, the servants were considered as human beings first and employees second – and he managed to induce a promise from one old shepherd to sing to him if he came to his cottage the following day.

Vaughan Williams duly arrived and put the man at his ease at once. Wearing his work clothes and on home ground, Mr Charles Pottipher immediately sang, unaccompanied, the song *Bushes and Briars* as many times as requested until his guest had written it all down. This was 'a revelation' as Vaughan Williams later wrote, the catalyst that he required. In those simple but natural surroundings, the fresh voice of English folk song was finally presented to him, not in any artificial way, but as the breath of a tradition that underpinned the formal art of that other England he knew: the ecclesiastical and choral music from the Tudors to Purcell. He could now see his way forward. He must find some way to draw these ancient strands together into a seamless flow.

'Bushes and Briars', as noted down by Vaughan Williams.

4 The Collector

The following two years were busy ones for Vaughan Williams. When he found time, he travelled like a man possessed from Essex and Norfolk to Yorkshire, back to Wiltshire and did not rest even when staying at Leith Hill Place, setting off instantly to scour Surrey and Sussex beyond. His preferred method of travel when he reached an area was either bicycling or walking and his gangling form with its rucksack containing his notebook and pencil became familiar and accepted. The countrymen he sought out were pleased to sing their old songs in surroundings they found comfortable, whilst the man who could enjoy a joke with them and drink a pint of ale copied them all down. Although he later admitted that it was not a very enjoyable task, possibly due to his basic shyness, and the general discomfort of lodgings, his direct method enabled him to collect the ancient words and music of ordinary English people with a new authenticity, so that when he joined the Folk Music Society in 1904 he was able to revive its stuffy image with research fresh from the fields.

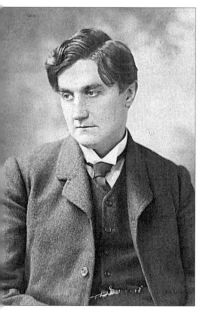

Ralph Vaughan Williams in 1903.

He shared his enthusiasm with Holst and introduced him to Cecil Sharp, who asked Holst to provide piano accompaniments for some of the tunes. This was still considered essential, although many of the originals had been sung unaccompanied. Indeed, one farm worker had told Vaughan Williams that, although it was nice for the singer to have a piano 'it does make it awkward for the listener.' Holst eventually arranged some suites of folk tunes, although he was of the opinion that 'the tunes are magnificent, but the words are unworthy' and was not as happy arranging the actual folk songs. He did agree with Vaughan Williams that the shape and idiom of this music helped to clarify his own, however, stripping it of the heavy chromaticism of Wagner.

Holst was not able to travel with his friend on his collecting expeditions due to his heavy work commitments, but Vaughan Williams was able to enlist the services of his younger contemporary George Butterworth who proved an equally enthusiastic researcher in the field. Eventually, they carried recording equipment with them – Edison Bell's disc phonograph, which, although ungainly, provided a useful talking point to break the ice and meant that the laborious task of writing down words and music could be postponed to a more convenient time. Vaughan Williams later wrote:

We were dazzled, we wanted to preach a new gospel, we wanted to rhapsodise on these tunes just as Liszt and Grieg had done on theirs ... we simply were fascinated by the tunes.

The more he collected, the more he was inspired, and the effect was immediately noticeable in his compositions at the time. Rhapsodies and tone poems appeared. The first to survive was 'A Symphonic Impression' entitled *In the Fen Country* in which Vaughan Williams did not actually quote a folk tune, but wrote his melodies in the style of folk music. This impressionistic portrait of the damp and chilly lowlands of East Anglia is the first work where Vaughan Williams's recognisable idiom may be heard breaking free from a Wagnerian stranglehold. It was followed by others including three Norfolk Rhapsodies where tunes he had collected from the fishermen of King's Lynn are quoted, but masterfully drawn into the texture of the music. He later revised these early works several times, a habit that he was to repeat with many of his compositions, and he eventually rejected the last two Norfolk Rhapsodies, but they still give an insight into the maturing of his musical mind. Here, at last, Vaughan Williams was close to achieving his ideal of 'a national English style ... modelled on the personal style of English musicians' with folk music absorbed as part of that style.

As well as travelling and collecting, Vaughan Williams also helped with a music festival his sister Meggie had founded with the aid of Lady Farrer, one of his friends from his student days at the Royal College of Music. The Leith Hill Festival, based largely in nearby Dorking, aimed to provide a platform for amateur choirs to compete with each other and then combine in a final concert; Vaughan Williams conducted them in the standard repertory as well as encouraging them to try out Elizabethan madrigals and church music. Although it seemed to have more enthusiasm than finance in its early years, the Festival was to grow into a respectable venue under Vaughan Williams's direction. He also became involved with Stratford-on-Avon where he arranged music for revivals of Shakespeare, Jonson and their contemporaries in Shakespeare's own town. A post teaching music at the James Allen's School for Girls in Dulwich lasted a year. He soon found it uncongenial, not only because of the headmistress's lack of commitment to music, but also due to petty restrictions which included the presence of a chaperone at every lesson he taught. Knowing that Holst and his wife Isobel were struggling to survive, he asked his friend to deputise for him and eventually to take over the job completely. This gave Vaughan Williams more time to devote to his researches, which entered a new phase when another strand was spun for the collector's web.

The Rev. Percy Dearmer, a clergyman of advanced views who was renowned for his work amongst the poor, commissioned Vaughan Williams to revise *Hymns Ancient and Modern*, the authorised hymn book of the Anglican Church. Cecil Sharp had recommended him and the radical clergyman was willing to overlook the composer's agnostic humanism. Vaughan Williams demurred at first but when he realised that this represented the musical wealth of what was yet another area of ordinary English experience, he was at last persuaded to accept. Many years later he gave a resumé of his intentions:

I decided, if I was to do the book at all I must be thorough, adventurous, and honest ... As regards honesty: the actual origin of the tune must be stated, and any alteration duly noted. But this does not mean that the original version must necessarily be adhered to. I always tried to find what I believed to be the best version ... Cecil Sharp had just made his epoch-making discovery of the beautiful melody hidden in the country-side: why should we not enter into our inheritance in the church as well as the concert room?

The task was only supposed to take a few months at most, but Vaughan Williams found so many variants and mistakes that it became obvious to him that it would take much longer. Although he did most of the work himself, he also asked Holst to help him and the two were soon busily immersed in cataloguing. Later Vaughan Williams wrote:

I wondered then if I was wasting my time. The years were passing and I was adding nothing to the sum of musical invention. But I know now that two years of close association with some of the best (as well as some of the worst) tunes in the world was a better musical education than any amount of sonatas and fugues.

The work indeed took two years and did not entirely rely on cataloguing what was already in existence. The two friends also incorporated folk tunes and provided some music of their own. The hymn tunes 'Come Down O Love Divine' (which he called 'Down Ampney' as a tribute to his father's church), 'For All The Saints' and five others are Vaughan Williams's compositions whilst that of the simple and beautiful carol 'In the Bleak Mid-winter' is Holst's. Other contemporary composers provided more. Vaughan Williams also uncovered many glories as he pieced the book together, including some of the greatest church music from the Elizabethans through to Purcell, but the most influential discovery for him was a psalm tune by the Elizabethan composer Thomas Tallis, 'When rising from the bed of death'. This haunted him for years and was eventually to provide inspiration for the *Fantasia on a theme by Thomas Tallis*, one of his finest works.

During this period Vaughan Williams was also asked to write incidental music for a dramatised production of Bunyan's *The Pilgrim's Progress* put on by amateurs at Reigate Priory near Dorking and was inspired to write the music by his contact with Bunyan's hymn 'Who would true valour see, let him come hither'. This would become almost an obsession that would continue to grow in his mind throughout his life.

Adeline Vaughan Williams in 1908.

Late in 1905, Ralph and Adeline had moved to number 13, Cheyne Walk, a substantial house in Chelsea: London's fashionably bohemian quarter. The historian Carlyle had lived in elegant Cheyne Walk, and in the redbrick streets behind writers including Wilde and Swinburne and artists such as members of the Pre-Raphaelite Brotherhood, Millais, Sickert and the English Impressionists had also lived. His contemporary neighbours included the Australian collector of folk song Percy Grainger, who soon became a valued colleague. The fine view across the Thames had often been painted, although Whistler's Impressionist-haze version of Battersea Bridge softened the fact that a short walk across it led to the slums of Battersea and that area of Lambeth where Vaughan Williams had encountered the 'louts' of St Barnabas, whilst South London stretched beyond into an ever-expanding suburbia that was obliterating rural Surrey. Chelsea lived in a bubble of artistic privilege, unreal, but soothing in its unreality. Here, Ralph and Adeline took on a married couple as housekeepers and had a garden for their cat. The location proved much more congenial than Westminster and gave Vaughan Williams the space he required.

In his study overlooking the Thames, Vaughan Williams worked steadily. He had begun a four-movement maritime symphony which he referred to in a letter to Holst as 'The Ocean'. He also continued work on *The English Hymnal*. During the time it had taken to complete, much of it had been funded by Vaughan Williams himself, but when it was published in 1906 it was an instant best-seller. This was probably due to Vaughan Williams's belief, laid out in the Preface, that 'it ought no longer to be true anywhere that the most exalted moments of the church-goer's week are associated with music that would not be tolerated at any place of secular entertainment ... A tune has no more right to be dull than to be demoralizing.' In addition to its popular appeal, the depth of its scholarship was to ensure that *The English Hymnal* made it the definitive hymn book of the Anglican Church, and it was to remain so for years to come.

The work had added a new dimension to the two composers' tireless search for an English idiom they could call their own, but at times they had felt the strain of so much church music and so many sacred texts, sensing they were having an adverse effect on their own compositions. At the end of 1904 as Vaughan Williams later wrote, 'Gustav and I were stuck so I suggested we should both set the same words in competition.' As relief from so much sacred music and as a way to get started again, they had each decided to compose a setting of Walt Whitman's 'Toward the Unknown Region', an extract from his *Whispers of Heavenly Death*. In this mystical but also firmly secular text the poet dares his soul to 'walk toward the Unknown Region'. When they had finished the exercise they compared their compositions during one of their 'field days' and decided that Vaughan Williams's was the more successful. Holst may have been over-sensitive, knowing that his previous attempts to set Walt Whitman had been comparative failures, but the manuscript that has survived shows it to have been an oddly mawkish exercise that was justifiably abandoned when he compared it with Vaughan Williams's. Some commentators have detected the influence of Brahms in Vaughan Williams's version and it is difficult not to think of that composer's *Song of Destiny* when hearing the opening bars. The formal structure of hymn tunes is also never far from the surface, but it is a fine piece nonetheless, moving easily from a questioning mystical intensity to affirmation as the soul bursts forth 'in Time and Space', and it was instantly accepted when Vaughan Williams offered it for the Leeds Festival in 1907. He conducted its first performance there in October and it was so well received that one critic singled him out as 'the foremost of the younger generation' of English composers.

Despite this accolade, Vaughan Williams was still insecure. Perhaps his immersion in English church music and folk song had caused him to suspect his music lacked lightness or, as he put it, 'In 1908 I came to the conclusion that I was lumpy and stodgy, had come to a dead-end, and that a little French polish would be of use to me', so he decided to study once more, this time in Paris with Maurice Ravel. Ravel was a few years younger than Vaughan Williams but had achieved more notable success and his mastery of orchestration was unbeaten. The two composers could not have been more different (Ravel small, neat and fastidious, Vaughan Williams large and untidy with a bluff forthrightness that proclaimed his Englishness) and their first meeting was a little uncertain. Ravel asked Vaughan Williams to write 'a little minuet in the style of Mozart'. Vaughan Williams quite forcefully rebuffed this request in his best schoolboy French. After that, as Vaughan Williams wrote:

... we became great friends and I learnt much from him. For example that the heavy contrapuntal Teutonic manner was not necessary ... He showed me how to orchestrate in points of colour rather than in lines.

Ravel set exercises in orchestration which Vaughan Williams worked on in the comfort of his room at the Hôtel de l'Univers et du Portugal. Ravel also introduced him to the music of the Russian nationalist school for the first time. Rimsky-Korsakov and Mussorgsky had done for their own country's folk music exactly what Vaughan Williams and his colleagues were doing for English music, only they had done it much earlier, and this must also have encouraged Vaughan Willliams. He wrote to Holst, '... it is doing me just the good I hoped it wd. – I go to him 4 or 5 times a week' and when he returned to London three months later the influence of the French 'Impressionist' composers was marked. The first music he wrote shows this quite distinctly, 'I came home with a bad attack of French fever,' he admitted, 'and wrote a string quartet which caused a friend to say that I must have been having tea with Debussy, and a song cycle with several atmospheric effects ...'

Things French were much in vogue at the time. Edward VII, aware that the much-vaunted 'splendid isolation' of the British Empire left it vulnerable to the brash expansionism of Germany with its demands for 'a place in the sun', visited Paris and signed the *Entente Cordiale* as a loose treaty with the French designed to exclude the German Kaiser from military and colonial expansion. Ravel stayed with Ralph and Adeline in April 1909, enjoying the sights with his hosts, and Debussy was also in London on various occasions conducting his *Nocturnes* and the hypnotically sensuous music drama *Pelléas et Mélisande* to rapturous applause at Covent Garden.

Vaughan Williams's *String Quartet No.1 in G minor* does have passing resemblances to the Debussy quartet, but this attractive work nonetheless contains folk-style passages and shows a real maturity and confidence in the handling of its material. The song cycle *On Wenlock Edge* set six poems from A.E. Housman's *A Shropshire Lad* for tenor, piano and string quartet. Here, the style achieves the lightness Vaughan Williams had been seeking, and manages to integrate his new techniques with the thoroughly English atmosphere of the poems. The work was hailed as a masterpiece of concentrated drama when first performed in November by the tenor Gervase Elwes – an artiste who was to make the work especially his own. Although the donnish and unmusical Housman later disagreed with various cuts Vaughan Williams had made in the texts, demanding, 'How would he like it if I cut two bars from his music?', Vaughan Williams was adamant that he had done the poet a favour by removing lines such as, 'The lads play heart and soul;/The goal stands up, the keeper/Stands up to keep the goal.'

'My French fever soon subsided,' Vaughan Williams wrote, 'but left my musical metabolism, on the whole, healthier,' and he was soon busy with other works that were firmly in the English tradition. Undergraduates at Cambridge frequently performed the plays of Ancient Greece in the original language as part of their Classical studies, and incidental music was usually provided by a composer with connections with the university. Stanford had provided music for tragedies by Aeschylus – *The Eumenides*, and Sophocles – *Oedipus Tyrannus*, whilst Parry's music for *Agamemnon* was contrasted with that in a lighter vein written for the bawdy satires of Aristophanes. *The Frogs, The Clouds, The Arcanians* and *The Birds* had all received this treatment and when *The Wasps* was suggested, Vaughan Williams was asked to write the music.

'The Wasps' are Athenians who have nothing better to do than sit on juries bringing in 'guilty' verdicts for cash. One old juror is deflected from this dangerous obsession by his son, who sets up a mock trial at home in which the dog is tried for stealing a cheese but calls kitchen implements as witnesses for his defence.

Vaughan Williams obviously warmed to the task and set to with gusto, writing an overture in which a buzzing sound as of angry insects gives way to infectiously humorous and masterfully orchestrated themes obviously influenced by English folk music. These were to be very English Greeks. The rest of the music for the play includes choruses, melodramas, entr'actes and dances, all written in the same humorous vein, as may be judged from the title of one mock-heroic item: *March-Past of the Kitchen Utensils*. The whole piece ends with a raucous romp in which the chief prop would have been a phallus in Ancient Greece. Even in the liberal atmosphere of Cambridge, that would have been going too far so the play ends with a general dance. The music was a great success when *The Wasps* was performed that year, and Vaughan Williams later arranged a suite from it, but it is the overture that went on to become one of his most popular and enduring early works.

This must have provided welcome relief from the other task Vaughan Williams was engaged on at the time. 'The Ocean', now renamed *A Sea Symphony*, like *Toward the Unknown Region* which may almost be regarded as an offshoot, is based on texts by Walt Whitman and is firmly in the tradition of English choral symphonies of the time. Works in this vein were regularly performed at the great English provincial choral festivals of which the Three Choirs Festival held in late summer alternately at Hereford, Gloucester and Worcester cathedrals was perhaps the most prestigious, and, by choosing this genre for his symphony, Vaughan Williams was treading on safer ground than if he had chosen the purely orchestral way. The work occupied him from 1903 to 1909. In October 1907 Vaughan Williams played it over to Delius, who was in London for performances of his Piano Concerto and *Appalachia*, and he later gave an account of their meeting:

I burst in on the privacy of Delius … and insisted on playing the whole of my Sea Symphony to him. Poor Fellow! How he must have hated it. But he was very courteous and contented himself with saying, 'Vraiment il n'est pas mesquin' [It's certainly not paltry].

It was not Delius but Stanford who helped get the composition accepted for performance at the 1910 Leeds Festival. But another work Vaughan Williams had also just finished was to upstage it only one month earlier.

5 New Voices From Old

It was typical of Vaughan Williams's subtly unorthodox career that his most characteristic and forward-looking work to date should be based on a piece written three hundred and fifty years before and in a form more associated with that age. He had worried for five years at the psalm by Thomas Tallis he had collected for *The English Hymnal,* using it first in the incidental music he had written for the amateur production of Bunyan's *The Pilgrim's Progress* and finally producing a single-movement work based on its haunting modal theme. He scored the *Fantasia on a Theme by Thomas Tallis* for String Quartet and Double String Orchestra, like the earlier *Introduction and Allegro* of Elgar, but it could not be more different. Whereas Elgar busily rushes his musical ideas to a climax, Vaughan Williams presents a meditation on the great Elizabethan theme using sonorous effects that are the culmination of his long love affair with cathedral acoustics and his knowledge of the effects achieved by divided strings.

The first performance took place in September 1910 at the Three Choirs Festival which had commissioned the work and it made a tremendous impression. A contemporary composer of church music, Herbert Howells, was present and wrote later:

Two thousand people were in Gloucester Cathedral that night, primarily to hear *Gerontius.* But there at the rostrum towered the unfamiliar magnificent figure [of Vaughan Williams]. He and a strangely new work for strings were between them and their devotion to Elgar.

Gloucester Cathedral photographed in the early twentieth century.

The two works performed that evening complemented each other in some measure. Elgar's great oratorio represents an orthodox Catholic mysticism whereas Vaughan Williams's *Tallis Fantasia* represents the more restrained but no less pure mysticism of the Anglican church. The older composer's work also shows that great English music could still speak through the German textures it had embraced, but what Vaughan Williams was showing was a way forward in which a different greatness could be achieved based on entirely English models.

Elgar's First Symphony had been performed in 1908 and had been hailed as the greatest work of its kind by an Englishman. Its nobility and breadth ensured that it was performed round the world more than a hundred times in that same year, and its basic optimism seemed to capture the confidence of the Edwardians as they gazed on their empire and their status as a world power. It

The composer conducts his *Sea Symphony* at Leeds in 1910.

was to Elgar they looked as their 'Minstrel of Empire' and he provided them with their 'pomp and circumstance' and their anthems of expansion. 'Wider still and wider' it seemed their bounds would always be set. But Vaughan Williams's nationalism was of a different order and he did not attempt to compete with such jingoism.

In 1910, Edward VII died. Elgar was completing his second and final symphony, dedicated to the memory of the dead king, the slow movement of which might be regarded as the swansong of the Edwardian era itself. Vaughan Williams provided something for a new age. His first symphony was not even billed as that when it was performed under his baton at the Leeds Festival on his thirty-eighth birthday, but *A Sea Symphony*, although choral from beginning to end, observes symphonic structure albeit in an unorthodox way. There is sonata form in the first movement, a slow movement, scherzo and finale and it does have many boisterous and confident moments, especially where sea shanties are quoted, yet the nature of Whitman's texts is cosmic, dealing with the mysterious uncertainties of life, and Vaughan Williams provides music with an appropriate mystical feel. This symphony gazes at the sea but realises it is a symbol for the infinite. In the slow movement, entitled 'On the Beach at Night Alone', the poet thinks of 'the clef of the universes' and of all the possibilities of unnamed worlds beyond. In the last movement, he considers the 'vast Rondure, swimming in space, covered all over with visible power and beauty ... and the teeming spiritual darkness' and wonders 'Wherefore unsatisfied soul? and whither O mocking life?' His answer lies in a mystical union between the soul and centre 'shedding forth universes' and ends with the poet steering 'for the deep waters only'.

The work received 'a very doubtful reception' according to Vaughan Williams, but his friend Hugh Allen 'at once arranged performances at Oxford and in London, though he confessed to me afterwards that he was rather frightened about it.' These performances confirmed the stature of the work. Parry was so impressed that he wrote in his diary, 'This is big stuff – with some impertinences'. It was the kind of impertinence that complacent England needed.

Vaughan Williams's interest in mysticism may have been fuelled by Holst's similar interests, and it is significant that the most mystical parts of the symphony are set to words taken from Whitman's 'Passage to India', but this is no borrowing of emotions for effect. That deep vein of spiritual mysticism was part of Vaughan Williams's character as surely as the bluff and dismissive manner with which he affected to brush it all away. It returns many times in his works. The *Tallis Fantasia* in which he saw the roots of Bunyan's Englishness as surely as those of the great Elizabethan composer Tallis, and the symphony in which he and Whitman seem to have been made for each other, are only two examples of this area of the man. In the end the ascent of the soul into truth is handled with as much ecstatic rapture as the ascent of Gerontius into a Catholic Heaven. Yet Vaughan Williams's rapture is agnostic and as such seems more in accord with the questioning nature of the twentieth century than Elgar's could ever have been.

The Coronation of George V produced the usual imperial pageantry, with the more established musicians such as Parry and Elgar providing music, although an Empire Exhibition with contributions from Britain's colonies and dominions also offered opportunities, and Holst was able to write music for a Pageant of London held at the Crystal Palace, together with arrangements of folk songs for brass band. A royal progress then followed through the Empire to reinforce British world status. Although radical ideas fermented beneath this world of Establishment protocol, it was clear that rebels would not be tolerated in the musical world. The atheism of Delius's great humanist *Mass of Life* had proved a stumbling block to its acceptance and, although railing at Stanford, Parry, *et al.*, declaring that they would hypocritically 'set the Bible to music' in order to maintain their positions, he was still a composer in exile from the musical establishment of his native land. The Devil may have the best tunes, but in England God still had the best words and, in order to progress, an English composer such as Vaughan Williams had to subdue his doubts to the Liturgy.

With works to his credit that had finally brought him to national attention as a force to be reckoned with, and commissions following for more Three Choirs Festivals, Vaughan Williams continued to mine the tradition of English mystical writing. He felt it prudent, however, to make his settings from more orthodox

Worcester Cathedral, early twentieth century.

religious texts, so chose poems by the Metaphysical religious poet George Herbert for his *Five Mystical Songs*. When they were first performed in Worcester in September 1911, they were praised by the music historian and critic of *The Times*, H.C. Colles, who recognised their visionary quality as mysticism 'not with the mystery of complexity which leads to confusion but with the deepest kind which is compatible with simplicity.' He also composed *Four Hymns* for tenor and wrote a *Fantasia on Christmas Carols* which was performed at Hereford in 1912. This incorporated some well-known carols, but also one Vaughan Williams had collected himself ('On Christmas night').

Secular works included another example of chamber music. He wrote his *Phantasy Quintet* for strings at the request of the patron W.W. Cobbett, a wealthy amateur musician who had instituted a prize for English composers. This stipulated that the entrant should write one-movement chamber pieces including the word 'Phantasy' in homage to the great instrumental 'Fancies' or 'Fantasias' originating in the Elizabethan age and developed throughout the seventeenth century by composers who included Byrd, Gibbons, Lawes and Purcell. The original structure progressed from section to section, building on material stated at the outset, and this is the form that Cobbett attempted to revive. Amongst the winners of his competition since its inauguration in 1905 were John Ireland, who had been Vaughan Williams's friend at the Royal College of Music, and other composers of the same generation including Frank Bridge and Herbert Howells and there is no doubt that the inspiration of these earlier models enriched twentieth century English music as composers became more aware of their roots. Vaughan Williams's piece is an attractive addition to the canon and would have been a labour of love, given the interest he had in the music on which the form was based. These works only added to his growing reputation, but he was also busy with more ambitious projects.

George Butterworth had once brusquely remarked 'you know, you ought to try your hand at a symphony,' and Vaughan Williams now took up his suggestion, expanding an idea for a tone poem on London into a purely orchestral work in this style. Nothing if not ambitious, he felt able at last to do justice to large canvases depicting great English themes. The tribute to the sea surrounding the island would be followed by a symphony celebrating its capital, still the world's largest city. In addition, he decided at last to try his hand at opera. Given the experiences of Holst, who had failed to make any impression with his own operas to date, and given also the lack of any genuine operatic tradition in England, this was a bold step. Vaughan Williams had previously attempted to write an opera based on Matthew Arnold's poem, *The Scholar Gypsy* but had not found this sufficiently dramatic a subject. His incidental music made him no stranger to the stage, however, and he now felt confident enough to break new ground basing his efforts on English influences, whereas Holst had preferred

44

to take his inspiration largely from Indian texts.

He had a plot based on English village life, and several well-formed ideas and key scenes in his mind, when he asked the editor of *The Times Literary Supplement* to find him a librettist: 'I want to set a prize fight to music,' he had said. When the *Times* journalist Harold Child was suggested, Vaughan Williams gave him strict instructions. This was to be 'an opera on more or less accepted lines and preferably a *comedy*, to be full of tunes, and lively, and one tune that will really *come off* ...' He may have had ballad operas such as Gay's *The Beggar's Opera* in mind, but he was also aware of the German tradition and that of other European folk operas, which he must Anglicize if he was going to avoid pastiche and invidious comparison. 'This fitted in with another idea of mine,' he wrote to Child,

which was to write a musical, what the Germans call 'Bauer Comedie' [Peasant Comedy] – only applied to English country life (real as far as possible – no sham) – something on the lines of Smetana's *Bartered Bride* – for I have an idea an opera written to *real* English words, with a certain amount of *real* English music and also a real English subject might just hit the right nail on the head ... the whole thing might be folk song-y in character, with a certain amount of 'real' ballad stuff thrown in.

How could Harold Child reconcile these demands? He was more used to reviewing exhibitions in London's art galleries. Like most people of his class, his view of the villagers of England was at best sentimental, at worst ignorant. When his libretto for *Hugh the Drover* was finished, it appeared adequate, but stale and patronising: the 'real' English words Vaughan Williams had demanded were not there. Vaughan Williams tactfully changed a great deal of it, perhaps recalling his thoughts published in *The Vocalist* in 1902:

Ideas in a musical drama must be such as a man can feel, and not such as he can only intellectually perceive ... the one thing that is not wanted for a musical drama is 'musical verse'. A decorative scheme of artificial metres and rhymes makes the most unsuitable word-book imaginable. That librettists of all times and countries have hailed from Grub Street, is a truism of musical history: but, contemptible as nearly all librettos are, their real defect lies in their utter unsuitability for musical treatment, both in subject and in style ...

The plot, set during the Napoleonic War and involving the love between a wandering free spirit, Hugh, and a village girl he wins from a bullying rival, may seem artificial and even sentimental but only if we regard Stevenson's *Songs of Travel*, Housman's *Shropshire Lad* and the novels of Richard Jefferies in the same light. These were Vaughan Williams's contemporaries whose writings represented an idealised view of rural existence based on known facts. Vaughan Williams was also an admirer of Thomas Hardy and his comparatively unsentimental view of rural com-

Vaughan Williams in 1911.

munities, whose epic poem, *The Dynasts*, set in the Napoleonic Wars, had just been published. Vaughan Williams also injected real folk music and its idioms into the situations Child had created and added others from his own experience. In addition to his prize fight, which is a technically brilliant piece of ensemble writing, incidents and anecdotes he had heard in country pubs and references to the surviving pagan customs of rural England were included. Whilst celebrating the Morris dancers and Maying ceremonies, however, he makes no excuse for the dangerous ignorance of the people who turn on Hugh when whipped up into patriotic frenzy. In the end, *Hugh the Drover* must be considered as fresh and convincing as the conventions of opera could allow, and remains as English as *Cavalleria Rusticana* is Italian.

He was also busy with other projects. He helped Holst bring music to the less-advantaged workers' institutes at Morley College, copying parts of the manuscript for Purcell's *Fairy Queen* so that they could give the first performance since Purcell's own time. This great undertaking helped consolidate the reputation of the seventeenth-century composer who was both admired so greatly and yet still so little known amongst his countrymen.

These were years largely given over to composing feverishly, occasionally teaching, and helping to organise and conduct the annual Leith Hill Festival, but Vaughan Williams also found time to sit on the committee of the English Folk Dance Society set up in 1911, believing that he might help guide its efforts towards the more authentic areas of collecting. Not that he was unaware of continental trends. Music given in London at this time included symphonies by Mahler and Sibelius and seasons of Diaghilev's *Ballets Russes* with their exotic Russian music, their barbarically colourful designs by Bakst and the legendary dancing of Nijinsky, which inspired a vogue for all things Russian. Vaughan Williams met Diaghilev and there were discussions with the great impresario about a possible collaboration, although these came to nothing. More exotic if more unconventional dancing was supplied by Isadora Duncan, who became a personal acquaintance and for whom Vaughan Williams sketched a choral ballet based on the wildly pagan Dionysiac revels of Euripides' *The Bacchae*, although this also came to nothing. On safer ground, he continued his work as musical arranger to the annual Shakespeare Festival in Stratford-on-Avon, and in this capacity he was able to use some of Holst's folk-inspired music in various plays.

By 1913, he had finished his second symphony, now called *A London Symphony* and it was scheduled for performance the following year. He had nearly completed *Hugh the Drover* although his attempts to find a venue for that were more problematic. He began work in 1914 on a tone poem for violin and orchestra, based on a poem by George Meredith, *The Lark Ascending*, written for the violinist Marie Hall. This, eventually to become one of his most popular works, would not see the light of day for another six years.

Vaughan Williams now felt confident enough to nail his colours to the mast in a series of articles for the Royal College of Music magazine entitled bullishly 'Who Wants the English Composer?' in which he makes much of a composer's duty to express the life of his own community with a 'sense of musical citizenship'. To do this he must reject European influences from the past:

We English composers are always saying, 'Here are Wagner, Brahms, Grieg, Tchaikovsky, what fine fellows they are, let us try and do something like this at home', quite forgetting that the result will not sound at all like 'this' when transplanted from its natural soil. It is all very well to catch the prophet's robe, but the mantle of Elijah is apt, like all second-hand clothing, to prove the worst of misfits.

The first performances of *A London Symphony* took place on 27 March 1914 conducted by Geoffrey Toye. George Butterworth had helped with the preparation of the orchestral parts and the concert was made possible by a patron, Bevis Ellis, who financed several concerts for new English composers at this time. Delius's tone poem *In a Summer Garden* also received a performance on this occasion and Ravel's *Valses Nobles et Sentimentales* were played in the second half of the programme, providing an opportunity for the audience to compare Vaughan Williams with his former tutor, an opportunity that many took to Ravel's disadvantage. The symphony was an instant success despite being over fifty minutes long, but Vaughan Williams was still not entirely happy with it and revised it at least twice over the years before being really satisfied, on one occasion cutting out what he called 'a dreadful hymn tune' in the middle of rehearsals. He also altered his programme notes for it as the revisions progressed, the most helpful being his last, in which he is at pains to stress the symphonic elements rather than the pictorial:

It has been suggested that this symphony has been misnamed, it should rather be called 'Symphony by a Londoner', that is to say it is in no sense descriptive, and though the introduction of the 'Westminster Chimes' in the first movement, the slight reminiscence of the 'Lavender City' in the slow movement, and the very faint suggestion of mouth organs and mechanical pianos in the Scherzo give it a tinge of 'local colour', yet it is intended to be listened to as 'absolute music'. Hearers may, if they like, localize the various themes and movements but it is hoped this is not a necessary part of the music. There are four movements: The first begins with a slow prelude; this leads to a vigorous allegro – which may suggest the noise and hurry of London, with its always underlying calm. The second (slow) movement has been called 'Bloomsbury Square on a November afternoon'. This may serve as a clue but is not a necessary 'explanation' of it. The third movement is a nocturne in the form of a Scherzo. If the hearer will imagine himself standing on Westminster Embankment at night, surrounded by the sounds of the Strand, with its great hotels on one side, and the 'New Cut' on the other, with its crowded streets and flaring lights, it may serve as a mood in which to listen to this music. The last movement consists of an agitated theme in three time, alternating with a march movement, at first solemn and later on energetic. At the end of this finale comes a suggestion of the noise and fever of the first movement – this time much subdued – then the 'Westminster Chimes' are heard once more: on this follows an 'Epilogue' in which the slow prelude is developed into a movement of some length.

In this symphony, Vaughan Williams was at last able to show his true city colours. He always considered himself a Londoner first, and a countryman second and it is significant that his first solely orchestral essay in this form should be based on the city he loved. In other ways it is a summing up of the influences that had shaped his style and points towards the symphonies to come. Folk music, impressionistic sketches and mystical intensity jostle harsh crescendi, dissonances and outbursts of tragic intensity. Holst attended the first performance and wrote to Vaughan Williams:

You have really done it this time. Not only have you reached the heights but you have taken your audience with you. Also you have proved the musical superiority of England to France. I wonder if you realized how futile and tawdry Ravel sounded after your Epilogue ... I wish I could tell you how I and everyone else was carried away on Friday. However it is probably unnecessary as I expect you know it already.

The Epilogue presents a portrait of the Thames, sweeping past London, and must have been influenced as much by Vaughan Williams's view from his Thames-side house as the literary source he later quoted: the closing pages of H.G.Wells's novel *Tono Bungay*. Here, the novelist sums up his portrait of London's complexity with the words '... the river passes – London passes, England passes ...' The Symphony is still a remarkable *tour de force* in its ability to integrate 'local colour' with deeply unnerving tragic moments. The sense of menace and unease that the music creates were being paralleled that time in Europe. Only three months after its first performance, an assassin's bullet in the Balkans unleashed the most terrible war the world had known and the complacency of Edwardian England was shattered for ever.

6 War

For more than a decade tensions had existed between the European empires. The alliance between Britain and France had been followed by one between France and Russia. Austria-Hungary had allied with the unstable German autocrat Wilhelm II so that the assassination of the Austrian heir to the throne on 28 June 1914 finally brought these tensions to a head. Exactly one month later Austria-Hungary declared war on Serbia, expecting an easy conquest, but this act set off the whole chain of alliances. Russia, the 'protector of the Slavs' came to Serbia's aid, Germany found a pretext to invade its old enemy France, entering the country through Belgium, and Britain joined the conflict on the side of Belgium and France. Soon, there was a general call for volunteers, with the famous poster of the imperial hero General Kitchener exhorting every man to aid his country. The nation was whipped up into a patriotic frenzy, while the British Army mobilised and began to leave for the battlefields of France in every available form of transport including omnibuses. The war, everyone confidently believed, would be over by Christmas. Many young composers rushed to join the ranks, including Holst and Vaughan Williams. Holst was turned down due to his short sight and neuritis, but Vaughan Williams, despite being forty-two and above the age of enlistment, was accepted. Music and the strenuous attempts to find a 'national voice' were shelved in the face of this danger to the nation itself.

News of defeats of the French and British forces at Mons and Le Câteau were followed by reports of a counter-offensive driving the Germans back to the River Marne. Here the worst aspect of this war was created: trenches were dug on both sides along a line from Verdun to the sea, and the opposing armies began a war of attrition involving four years of the most savage mechanised slaughter ever witnessed.

At first, Vaughan Williams saw no action. He was attached to a Special Constabulary unit in Chelsea with the rank of sergeant, but volunteered immediately for the Royal Army Medical Corps, being transferred to the London Field Ambulance unit shortly afterwards. His chosen rank of private showed that the had no intention of using his considerable influence to gain a comfortable position, and the training on Salisbury Plain was particularly arduous for a man of his age unused to physical hardship. He took it all in his stride, making friends with the younger men of his unit and cheerfully performing even the most lowly work

Vaughan Williams and his
RAMC ambulance are on the
right of the picture.

in the camps. He was untidy, but made an especial friend of Harry
Steggles, a Cockney soldier who helped him pass muster on parade
and sang raucous music hall songs to the troops with his famous
companion providing the piano accompaniment. 'When father
papered the parlour, you couldn't see him for paint' was a particular favourite. From Chelsea, they were transferred to Dorking
where Vaughan Williams kept morale high by organising camp
concerts and a military band, although he encouraged more
serious music-making by forming a choir and small groups of
instrumental performers. He played the organ at unit church
services, occasionally mischievously improvising voluntaries on
music hall songs, and was finally sent to Audley End Park hospital
as wagon orderly where he had a brief respite from camp conditions, being billeted with a household of amateur musicians.

Two years passed in this way, with parades and all the other
tedious army ritual relieved only by his wife's occasional visits
and leave in London. But the city in wartime did not have much
to recommend it, and musically there was little to distract him.
Most of his musical colleagues were engaged in war-work and
there was an oppressive atmosphere of jingoism and propaganda
all around, with women handing out white feathers to any young
man not in uniform, and Germans, the people whose civilisa-
tion all aspiring composers had admired, being guyed as child-
bayoneting barbarians. His wife was also growing increasingly ill,
her arthritis making the large house in Cheyne Walk a burden,
so that his visits home provided little relief from the stressful,
stultifying effects of the conflict. This seems to have caused an
inspirational block, and he wrote no new music, although a
performance of the *London Symphony* in 1915 under Dan Godfrey
caused him to have second thoughts and he set about revising
that. Only Holst, whom he still saw when he could, provided any
encouragement. Holst continued to work at St Paul's School and
Morley College where he produced festivals of English music.
He had also found a house in Thaxted, Essex, and was busily

establishing a series of Whitsun concerts there. He was writing too, composing what would become his most famous work, *The Planets* suite.

In June 1916, Vaughan Williams was finally posted to France, and felt at last that he was about to be of some real use. Holst had written him a letter detailing his own musical activities and Vaughan Williams replied enthusiastically before leaving:

We are on the eve – all packed and ready – I can't say more – write to me occasionally, my wife will give you the address.

Your letter about Thaxted was splendid – I sometimes feel that the future of musical England rests with you – because every Paulina who goes out, & for the matter of that every Morleyite, will infect 10 others & they in their turn will infect 10 others – I will leave you to make the necessary calculations.

Good luck to you – I feel that perhaps after the war England will be a *better* place for music than before – largely because we shan't be able to buy expensive performers etc. like we did. I wish I could have been there – perhaps next Whit: – who knows? I read your letter over & over again, it was so inspiriting – We don't take music as part of our everyday life half enough – I often wish we could all migrate to some small town where there could really be a musical community – London is impossible from that point of view.

Organising military music in 1915.

51

On the front line, World War I.

At last Vaughan Williams saw the war at first hand. As an ambulance orderly, he was providing humanitarian aid to his suffering comrades, as was his teacher Ravel who was acting as an ambulance driver for the French troops at the same time, although the two did not meet. This seemed to be more in keeping with his ideals. He performed his duties with great bravery, but what he saw could not but scar a sensitive man emotionally: the numbing trench slaughter continued relentlessly, the sky was filled with the screams of shells and the flashes of explosions, the conditions in the trenches were indescribably squalid, whilst all around desolate wastelands punctured by mud craters that could swallow horses and men stretched as far as the eye could see. The Battle of the Somme and the year-long Battle of Verdun saw the greatest slaughter. Although the Germans were driven a little further back, the offensive made little real impact and the stalemate continued. Vaughan Williams heard of the deaths of several colleagues, including his close friend George Butterworth on the Somme, and wrote to Holst:

... I've indeed longed to be home in many ways during the last month but in other ways I should not like to come home for good till everything is over, or in some other normal way.

Remember me to all the Morleyites and wish them good luck from me – I shall think of all your schoolgirls on All Saints Day.

I sometimes dread coming back to normal life with so many gaps – especially of course George Butterworth – he has left most of his MS to me – & now I hear that [Bevis] Ellis is killed – out of those 7 who joined up together in August 1914 only 3 are left – I sometimes think now that it is wrong to have made friends with people much younger than oneself – because soon there will be only the middle aged left – & I have got out of touch with most of my contemporary friends – but then there is always

52

I am quite well.

I have been admitted into hospital

{ sick — and am going on well,

wounded } and hope to be discharged soon.

I am being sent down to the base.

I have received your { letter dated

telegram „

parcel „

Letter follows at first opportunity.

I have received no letter from you

{ lately

{ for a long time.

A MERRY X MAS

Signature
only R V Williams

Date Dec 8 — 1916

[Postage must be prepaid on any letter or post card
addressed to the sender of this card.]

W3107/293   2246   800m.   9/15.   C. & Co., Grange Mills, I.W.

A message from the Front.

you & thank Heaven we have never got out of touch & I don't see why
we ever should.

Reading Vaughan Williams's reference to the normal round of
music-making in his friend's charge, it is possible to feel his
yearning for an England that seemed so far from the horrors of
the Western Front that it was almost an idealised country of the
mind. As his ambulance drove from the battlefield to the hospital
loaded with its maimed and dying young men, he began to dream
of such an England, not 'lambkins frisking, as most people take
for granted' as he put it, but a landscape that had been internalised
in the poems of George Herbert, the mystical writings of Bunyan
and Blake and the paintings of Samuel Palmer. The catalyst occurred when, as he wrote: '… I used to go up night after night with
the ambulance wagon at Ecoivres and we went up a steep hill and
there was a wonderful Corot-like landscape in the sunset …'

This and a bugle call he heard which seemed to epitomise lone-
liness and longing were the sparks that set him writing again.
From the noise and shambles of the battlefield with all its sense-
less waste, he brought the healing processes of the imagination
to bear in sketches for a third symphony, eventually to be called
A Pastoral Symphony.

At the end of 1916, his unit was posted to Greece. The Allies
were fighting a front against the moribund Ottoman Empire in
the Dardanelles to the south, but Vaughan Williams was closer to
Constantinople, in Salonica. Here despite the ramshackle appearance of a city ravaged by fire, he could enjoy a little of Greek life,
watching and noting down folk songs and dances. From there
they were posted to a region close to Mount Olympus, but the
awe-inspiring sight of the home of the Gods was little comfort to
mere mortals throughout the bitterly cold and boring winter
spent on its slopes. Privates Vaughan Williams and Steggles
huddled in a draughty tent warmed only by braziers improvised
from old tins, although this did not entirely dampen their spirits
and Vaughan Williams later recounted how he had organised the
singing of carols at Christmas under the shadow of the myth-
inspiring mountain. They were eventually moved nearer the
fighting, but at this point the Powers That Be decided that Vaughan
Williams was being wasted, due to his background and upbring-
ing (not, it should be noted, due to his fame as a composer) and
he was sent for officer training.

Vaughan Williams was distinctly unhappy about this. Later
commentators have blamed most of the protracted bungling of
World War I on the decisions of generals and officers far from the
Front whose chief distinction was that they were drawn from the
public school 'officer classes'. The ordinary soldiers were 'lions'
but in the famous phrase, 'lions led by donkeys', and Vaughan
Williams instinctively concurred with this, but go he had to. He
said goodbye to his unit with some regret, promising to keep in
contact with them – a promise that he kept, especially in the case

of his friend Private Steggles and from August to November 1917, he underwent the necessary training in Uckfield, Sussex. From there he wrote to Holst:

I wish we could have met again – but I was bunged off here all in a hurry – I'm *in* it now, though we don't really start work until Friday – no leave till the middle of the course – about 2 months – it seems a fairly free and easy place at present, but a good deal of stupid ceremonial – *white gloves!!* (on ceremonial parades) (N.B. I believe there is a war on). I should have loved another long talk with you. Our house orderly is a funny little chap called Smith who has played with the 'worm' sort of orchestra (violin) all over the place, he was at the Royal College of Music 12 years ago ...'

At the end of the course, he was posted back to France as a Second Lieutenant in the Royal Garrison Artillery in charge of transport and musical recreation in Rouen. At this time, the German armies had made a breakthrough on the Marne and were bombarding Paris with their terrible long-range 'Big Bertha' cannon, yet by April they were being pushed back again and it seemed the conflict was reaching its final stages. Vaughan Williams heard that Holst had had to alter his name, from von Holst to Holst, in the general atmosphere of anti-German feeling in order to gain a musical post in a military capacity. By doing this, he was in illustrious company, the English Royal Family having already shed its German name, which became Windsor and Mountbatten in place of Saxe-Coburg-Gotha and Battenberg. The insults were, of course, mutual, Kaiser Wilhelm II frequently pointing to his withered arm and declaring it was the only part of him that was English! Vaughan Williams wrote to Holst:

141 Heavy Bty, BEF France

I wonder if you will go to Holland – I shd feel more inclined for the naval job myself – but still there is the 3rd alternative I hope, of your stopping at Morley – when all this is over it will I believe be the people who've kept the lamp alight who will count as the heroes.

The war has brought me strange jobs – can you imagine me in charge of 200 horses!! That's my job at present – I was dumped down into it straight away, and before I had time to find out which were horses and which were wagons I found myself in the middle of a retreat – as a matter of fact we had a very easy time over this – only one horse killed so we were lucky.

At present I am down near the sea undergoing a 'gunnery course' – more of a rest that anything else – but it's given me an opportunity of learning something about my gun (among other things.) Having been trained as a 6" Howitzer man I've been bunged into a 60 pdr!

I wish I could have been at Thaxted – but that will come after the war – I shd be very sorry for you to leave Morley & Thaxted and all that – but it would be interesting to see if you have established a tradition & if it will carry on without you.

Let me have a letter when you can. What are you writing?

Yours

RVW

Holst was writing his extraordinary choral work *The Hymn of Jesus* based on the his own translations of Apocryphal Greek biblical texts at this time, and only a few months later, in September, a private performance of *The Planets* was given at the Queen's Hall under Adrian Boult; however, Vaughan Williams was unable to attend this momentous first performance. In late October Holst too was on his way to Salonica in charge of music for the forces, although nominally attached to the YMCA. Vaughan Williams remained in France where the Germans finally surrendered unconditionally in November, worn out by the struggle. He wrote to Holst:

I am still out here – slowly trekking towards Germany, not a job I relish, either the journey or its object. I've seen Namur and Charleroi and was disappointed in both – every village we pass is hung with flags and triumphal arches ...

We usually march about 10 kilos or more a day and rest every 4th day – it's a tiresome job watering and feeding horses in the dark before we start... Then usually 2 or 3 wagons stick fast in the mud on the first start off and worry and delay ensues, and finally when one gets to one's destination one has to set up one's horse lines and find water and fill up nose bags etc. and if *this* has to be done in the dark it beggars description – so you see there's not much music-writing going at present. But I've started a singing class and we are practising Xmas carols and 'Sweet and Low'.

He stayed until February 1919, then officially appointed Director of Music to the First Army, in charge of education and musical activities whilst the army was slowly demobilised. As with everything he did, he brought enthusiasm to the task, teaching and leaving behind an orchestra and several choirs when he returned to England. Holst was still in Greece, where he seems to have had a happier and more inspiring time than Vaughan Williams. He wrote enthusiastically of the concerts he had organised under difficult conditions and of his joy at seeing the Byzantine splendours of Constantinople, and Mount Olympus and Athens especially:

... I've learnt what 'classical' means. It means something that sings and dances through sheer joy of existence. And if the Parthenon is the only building in the world that does so, then there is only one classical building in the world.

All the old talk of classical v romantic used to irritate me but it is only now I realise what twaddle it is ...

... the first glimpse of [the Parthenon] after going through the Propylea was like love at first sight. One was reduced to idiocy. Again, I mean *I* was...

Elsewhere, meanwhile, it was not so easy to be enthusiastic. A new sense of inquiry was in the air following the Armistice, and old certainties were being questioned everywhere.

7 For the Healing of the Nations

The Kaiser was deposed and exiled but he was not the only emperor to lose his crown. The Czar of Russia and his family had been murdered and their country was taken over by Communists; Austria-Hungary was dissolved and the Emperor deposed; even Turkey's Sultan would eventually be replaced by a president with European ideas. New countries emerged from the old empires, hidden nationalities and languages reasserted themselves and with the new European order came the desire to throw off old values and experiment freely in the arts. Britain had emerged intact but exhausted, and only its Establishment seemed to be unchanged, yet that self-regarding mirror which had reflected Edwardian society's opulence now lay smashed in dangerous fragments before the survivors and a new mood of discontent ran beneath the bland assurances of its Victory celebrations.

The poets who had been caught up in the conflict were no longer concerned with Georgian nature worship, and they had raged against the brutality of mechanical warfare, their imagery stark and their vision uncompromising. Many had perished, together with other artists of great promise. Others were so disturbed by their ordeal that they would never recover: amongst them the poet and composer Ivor Gurney who gradually went insane. Vaughan Williams knew him, as he had known many of the war's victims and he had seen many of its horrors. He returned to an England less inclined to accept the cosy ideas of tradition and the past. Soon, the Suffragettes' cause would be vindicated and women, who had filled the civilian jobs during the war, would gain the vote and other basic rights. Demands would be made for better working conditions in a labour market drastically reduced by the slaughter of millions of young men, and in a few years a new agitation would produce the first Labour government, committed to social reform.

Although they still kept the house in Cheyne Walk, Ralph and Adeline moved to temporary lodgings in Sheringham, Norfolk, where Adeline was nursing her invalid brother. Ralph did not remain isolated from London, however, and he busied himself further in Dorking where the Leith Hill Festival was being revived after the War. He was also able to take up his manuscripts once more, collating new folk song arrangements for publication and revising *Hugh the Drover*. But he was beginning to fear he had become an Establishment figure. He received an honorary doctorate from Oxford University in June, an occasion when his *Sea*

Rehearsing at the first Leith Hill Musical Festival after the Great War.

Symphony was performed, but this honour only seemed to add further to the weight of his pre-war reputation. He had changed since then. How could he pick up the pieces and renew himself at the age of forty-seven?

He had the sketches for the symphony directly inspired by the war, and he began to shape these into an elegiac structure of deeply felt intensity. As his previous two symphonies had celebrated the sea and the capital, so his latest inhabited the English countryside, but not in any cliché-ridden sense. It grew from that sense of peace that follows exhaustion and desolation, and touched a nerve of English mysticism activating a process by which Vaughan Williams hoped the psyche of the nation might be made whole.

A new work by Elgar was performed in October 1919, which seemed to sum up the mood of the times. He described his *Cello Concerto* as 'a man's attitude to life' and since the music is almost unremittingly melancholy, that attitude could only be seen as the sad coda to a society that had fêted him as its principal musician. For the next fifteen years until his death, he would be virtually silent, retreating into his own complex, private world and leaving the reputation of English music in the hands of middle-aged composers such as Vaughan Williams and Holst, and the generation of as yet untried younger men.

The new generation found themselves being taught by Vaughan Williams and Holst. Parry had died the previous year and been replaced at the RCM by Vaughan Williams's old friend, Hugh Allen. New brooms sweep clean, and the new principal almost doubled his teaching staff overnight, bringing in Vaughan Williams and Holst to lecture in composition alongside their old master Stanford. Although Holst was a well-established teacher, with long and varied experience, Vaughan Williams had only taught occasionally and had no real methodology. He openly admitted to his students that he 'could teach them nothing, only encourage them', but his encouragement was such that he soon became respected and sought-after by them all. He later wrote: 'I always try to remember the value of encouragement. Sometimes a callow youth appears who may be a fool or may be a genius, and I would rather be guilty of encouraging a fool than of discouraging a genius.'

He believed that a composer could find himself through experimentation, as he had done, and distrusted textbook solutions and exercises. He suggested that his students should set up 'field days' amongst themselves such as he and Holst had benefited from and that they could learn more from other composers than from any teacher, but he also admonished them, 'never try to be original. If you are original you needn't try. If you aren't, no amount of trying will make you so.'

As he busied himself, the emotional scars began to heal and he was able to work on several compositions at the same time. In addition to the new symphony, he maintained the serene atmosphere by taking up some of the incidental music he had written in 1906 for Bunyan's *The Pilgrim's Progress* and working it up into a one-act opera entitled *The Shepherds of the Delectable Mountains*, based on the final episode where Christian (Pilgrim in Vaughan Williams's version) finally reaches the gates of the Celestial City after encountering all the trials of 'the wilderness of this world', and it may not be too fanciful to suggest that this too represented some cathartic form of healing for Vaughan Williams.

He was still not entirely happy with the *London Symphony* and subjected it to another revision and also took up his score for *The Lark Ascending* for violin and orchestra, which he had originally composed in 1914, and began to revise it whilst staying with friends in the Cotswolds. The poem by George Meredith on which it is based is partly inscribed on the score, and provides a further insight into the healing processes of Vaughan Williams's mind at the time, processes that produced one of the most lyrical and effective tone-poems in Vaughan Williams's output:

> He rises and begins to round,
> He drops the silver chain of sound,
> Of many links without a break,
> In chirrup , whistle, slur and shake ...
> For singing till his heaven fills,
> 'Tis love of earth that he instils,
> And ever winging up and up,
> Our valley is his golden cup
> And he the wine which overflows
> To lift us with him as he goes ...
> Till lost on his aerial rings
> In light, and then the fancy sings.

He also composed a *Mass in G Minor*. He had no qualms about liturgical settings, remarking that 'there is no reason why an atheist could not write a good Mass.' He had Holst's 'Morleyites' in mind, and whilst he was composing it he allowed the first performance of the 'Kyrie' to take place in the chapel of Alleyn's School in Dulwich where Holst was holding his Whitsun Festival that year. The music was also inspired by the Catholic cathedral at Westminster whose choirmaster, R.R. Terry, regularly employed music by the Elizabethans for liturgical use, the candlelit interiors of the Byzantine-style building providing a haunting setting for the music Vaughan Williams so greatly admired.

Holst had dedicated his own choral work *The Hymn of Jesus* to Vaughan Williams and when it was given its first public performance in 1920 it received immense critical acclaim. It had also excited its audience greatly; Vaughan Williams, who attended it, said afterwards, 'I wanted to get up and embrace everyone and then get drunk.' This was a different kind of sacred music from Vaughan Williams's. Holst's vision was more Byzantine, more Eastern Mediterranean, his text taken from the primitive writings of the earliest Christian traditions as found in the Apocrypha and his music representing the almost pagan vitality of prayer as dance. Vaughan Williams's Mass was rooted in the Elizabethan Anglican tradition with its cooler and more meditative mysticism. Although both works used plainsong as their starting points, they then went their separate ways. The mutual admiration Vaughan Williams and Holst had for each other's works shows they appreciated that the revitalisation of English music could contain such varying methods and still achieve something uniquely national. They both knew that English music was a broad church.

Yet for some young artists, both composers seemed irrelevant. They appeared to be middle-aged representatives of Elgar's pre-war generation and its inherent 'Romanticism'. This vague term was used to include folk song and the 'Celtic Twilight' of Arnold Bax and his followers and seemed a symptom of the greater sickness of nationalism that had caused the War in the first place. An artistic reaction accompanied the new political and social upheavals in Europe. Soon, 'neo-classicism', indulged in by Stravinsky, Hindemith and many other continental composers, would attempt to make music unemotional and objective. In Paris, Futurist and Dadaist artists indulged in open insult, displaying such objects as urinals and defaced masterpieces. Their exhibitions admitted the public through toilets, gave them hammers and encouraged them to smash up the exhibits. Film studios in Germany were producing their first silent Expressionist masterpieces while in England T.S. Eliot wrote his disturbing anti-epic *The Waste Land*. A new flippancy began to skate across the surface tension with 'flappers' in short skirts indulging in dance crazes, and an explosion of Jazz.

The younger English composers eventually flirted with these influences. Arthur Bliss, fresh from the front where he had lost a brother, reacted by indulging in anarchic rhythms with his Jazz-time *Rout* and the nonsense of *Madame Noy*. Constant Lambert eventually produced his *Rio Grande* in the same style, soon to be followed by a succession of witty ballets based on the French style of Jean Cocteau and *Les Six*. Lord Berners and William Walton catered for the new taste in brittle sensation, the latter collaborating with the literary Sitwells to produce *Façade* in a sitting room in Carlyle Square, a short walk from Vaughan Williams's house in Chelsea. Edith Sitwell's fantastical poems were declaimed through a megaphone attached to a hole in a curtain to the accompaniment of musical parodies. The whole 'entertainment' seemed to embody the spirit of an age which was at once popular and élitist, excitingly experimental, yet confused.

In this climate, Vaughan Williams's use of modal forms drawn from folk music and the rhythmic flexibility of Tudor sacred and secular music seemed faintly old-fashioned, but both he and Holst insisted on the importance of tradition in underpinning new developments. They were both aware of modern trends and studied them with interest, but believed that, if a composer was going to experiment with new ideas, it would be useful to have this firm basis, so they continued to teach and write accordingly.

As though to reinforce the solidity of new English music, a performance of the *London Symphony* in its revised edition was arranged by the new British Musical Society and given in the Queen's Hall in May 1920 conducted by Albert Coates. This version was published later in the year. Vaughan Williams was aware that it was a work that he had somehow outgrown, but he still regarded it with great affection and went on to produce a further revision at a later date. Years later he said, 'You know, this is my favourite symphony, but you must not tell anybody, because I am not supposed to like it.'

In addition, Holst was finally achieving the respect and adulation that Vaughan Williams had hoped for him throughout their long collaboration, and with the first complete public performance of *The Planets Suite* in late 1920, was sucked into a whirlwind of publicity and fame. But he heartily detested it, writing, 'It has made me realise the truth of "Woe to you when all men speak well of you" ... Every artist ought to pray that he might not be a "success". If he's a failure he stands a good chance of concentrating upon the best work of which he's capable.'

As well as quietly working on his *Pastoral Symphony*, Vaughan Williams continued with his revision of *Hugh the Drover*. It seemed possible that interest in opera might be developing in England with the formation of the British National Opera Company to rival the stranglehold Covent Garden had had on the medium. He was also encouraged by Holst, who was then writing a comic opera based on some parodies he had written for Morley College to be entitled *The Perfect Fool*, and the two composers hoped that their operas might eventually find a place in an emerging English repertoire. They still regularly met for their 'field days' when they had the time, despite being successful, as though they were unable to reconcile their public image with private insecurity and required the reinforcement of mutual help and respect.

In 1921, Adeline's brother died. She was now more than ever feeling below par, having lost her mother during the War and suffering herself with the arthritis which threatened to cripple her. Nevertheless, she and Ralph moved back to a more settled existence in Cheyne Walk, where she could still manage to climb the stairs, though with difficulty, and found some comfort from being surrounded by their old friends. They now shared the house with Adeline's sister Emmeline and her husband, a musician and lecturer colleague of Vaughan Williams's at the Royal College of Music who was always known for professional purposes as R.O. Morris. Vaughan Wiliams's life had begun to settle after the upheavals of the previous eight years: he was back in his work study in Chelsea with its view of the Thames and he had been appointed conductor of the Bach Choir at the Royal College of Music, succeeding Hugh Allen who had found that his administrative duties as Principal had begun to take up most of his time.

Ralph and Gustav on a walking tour. The picture was taken by W.G. Whittaker.

Vaughan Williams relished this as a way of introducing many new works to the public alongside the tried and tested repertoire of Bach. In June the first London performance of *The Lark Ascending* was given with its dedicatee, Marie Hall, taking the violin part. The rapt lyricism of this tone poem consolidated Vaughan Williams's reputation as a nature poet of supreme sensitivity.

In the autumn Vaughan Williams enjoyed a short holiday. The Three Choirs Festival had returned to Hereford Cathedral for the first time since the War and a performance of Holst's *Hymn of Jesus* was featured. Afterwards, Vaughan Williams joined Holst and his friend, the choirmaster W.G.Whittaker, and the three spent a week rambling through the nearby villages with views of the Malvern Hills in the distance. He had just finished the *Pastoral Symphony* and it was scheduled for performance in January the following year under Adrian Boult, a newly-emerged talent who had conducted a memorable performance of the *London Symphony* at the end of 1920 and who was also becoming known as a supreme interpreter of Holst's *Planets*.

A Pastoral Symphony was not appreciated by all who heard it. Nothing could have been as silly as the composer Peter Warlock's remark that it reminded him of 'a cow looking over a gate', but if the audience had expected a work similar to Beethoven's Sixth Symphony, they could not have been more bemused either. As Vaughan Williams wrote in the programme note, 'The mood of this Symphony is almost entirely quiet and contemplative', and, apart from a scherzo marked 'pesante' (firmly) that is exactly how the music progresses. Vaughan Williams was extending his technique into what has been called 'polymodality', but such terms might even confuse a listener searching for meanings. 'Pantheism' was another word used to describe the underlying sense of nature mysticism that some found in the music, and, like the state induced by the god Pan himself, it has moments of quiet awe and terror. There is a bugle call, a reminder of the War, but it is a distant, muted reminder played on what Vaughan Williams specified should be a 'natural' bugle, whilst the finale begins and ends with a wordless soprano who carries the music alone into silence. Yet this human voice is also unearthly, for neither people nor cows have a place in a landscape which is 'pastoral' distilled to its abstract essence. Perhaps the only comparison could be made with a similar movement in the Third Symphony of the Danish composer Carl Nielsen in which wordless voices intermingle with the orchestra to produce a similar sense of the mystical essence of nature. His symphony was written in 1910-11 but unlike his great Finnish contemporary, Sibelius, he was still unknown in England, so Vaughan Williams's effects must be considered as growing out of his own deep sense of appropriateness.

A few years later, Holst wrote to Vaughan Williams, 'I'm quite sure that I like the Mass and Pastoral Symphony best of all your things', and Herbert Howells wrote of the music: 'Tune never ceases. One after another come tributary themes, short in themselves, and so fashioned as to throw one into doubting their being new.' These tunes 'will not draw faces or produce crude pictures of craggy heights, but those of the Malvern Hills when viewed from afar.' It was this reticence the first audience found so disorientating when listening to this thoroughly original symphony. However, considering the circumstances in which it had been conceived, it may be regarded as the culmination of the self-healing process which Vaughan Williams had envisaged for the nation.

A Pastoral Symphony was performed several times that season and came to the attention of a wealthy American, Carl Stoeckel, founder of the Norfolk Connecticut Summer Festival. He was so interested that he invited Vaughan Williams to the USA to conduct the work in the spring. This was the first indication that his music was beginning to be noticed abroad and Vaughan Williams accepted.

Adeline and he made the long journey across the Atlantic by ocean liner, finding the tedium of the crossing worth the effort on arrival. Carl Stoeckel was the archetypal rich American patron and the couple wanted for nothing. Vaughan Williams was particularly impressed by New York, as skyscrapers were then an entirely American phenomenon. He wrote to Holst from the Plaza Hotel:

I have seen (a) Niagara, (b) the Woolworth building and am most impressed by (b). I've come to the conclusion that the Works of Man terrify me more than the Works of God. I told myself all the time that N'ga was the most wonderful thing in the world – and so it is – especially when you get right under it – but I didn't once want to fall on my knees and confess my sins – whereas I can sit all day and look out of my window (16 floors up) at the skyscrapers ...

By the way, my millionaire has put us up in the swaggerest hotel in N.Y. ... we were whirled off in a taxi and up 16 floors in an elevator – to a *suite* of rooms with *2 bathrooms* with this wonderful view all over N.Y. – then whirled down again into a sort of Cathedral where we had supper

(Chicken salad – oh, the American food – it's beyond powers of expression.) Then at 11, just as we were going to bed, the great man and his wife appeared – very nice and simple. But I never want a patron – it's too wearing.

I've come to the conclusion that N.Y. is a good place but wants hustling badly – the buses are slow and stop wherever you like – Broadway is I believe easier to cross than High Street, Thaxted.

We had two rehearsals of 1¼ hours as yet. I think I shall need all I shall get ...

Soon afterwards they arrived in Norfolk where Vaughan Williams conducted his *Pastoral Symphony* to an audience of 1500 people, many of them farmers and factory workers sitting on the lawns of the Stoeckels' estate, and a fine performance was applauded warmly. Ralph and Adeline were overwhelmed by the Stoeckels' hospitality. They stayed in their white colonial mansion with its fashionable 'English' style of living, and were entertained with rich food and wine. They were taken on excursions and met many people before being whisked off to Boston where they visited the Music Conservatoire. In fact, the whole trip was so minutely organised by the Stoeckels that Vaughan Williams began to feel restless and, although very grateful, was glad when the tour was complete, saying he knew how composers such as Mozart felt living under a patron.

In the summer, a private performance of *The Shepherds of the Delectable Mountains* was given in the Parry Memorial Theatre at the Royal College of Music with Queen Mary in the audience, and the *Mass in G Minor* was published with a dedication to 'Gustav Holst and his Whitsuntide Singers'. One of his students recalls that Holst cancelled his prepared lesson at the Royal College of Music after receiving the score and played the whole work through to them in his excitement. He had written to Vaughan Williams on its arrival the day before:

It arrived on Wednesday but I only got *It* yesterday and shall not be able to look at *It* properly until tomorrow morning.

... How on earth Morleyites are ever going to learn the Mass I don't know. It is quite beyond us but still further beyond us is the idea that we are not going to do it. I've suggested that they buy copies now and then when we meet in September I'll sack anyone who does not know it by heart!

I'm thinking that the best plan for next season will be to chuck JS [Bach] and at the first concert do a little Byrd and a little RVW – then at the summer concert do a little Byrd and a lot of RVW.

We are all tremendously proud of the dedication.

On 12 October 1922, Ralph and Adeline were awakened by singing coming from the small garden of their Cheyne Walk house. It was Holst and a few of their mutual friends performing a song specially written for Vaughan Williams's birthday. He was fifty years old.

8 'Drifting Apart'

Despite reaching his half century, Vaughan Williams was as energetic as he had been in former years. He continued to be busily involved in the Leith Hill Festival and plunged himself into education work, sitting on committees for the advancement of music teaching and using his influence with his brother-in-law, H.A.L. Fisher, on the Board of Education to ensure that folk singing and dancing were added to the curriculum in all schools. He was still active in the folk song movement and used a number of folk songs in the works he wrote the following year. These included a suite for military band, some arrangements of sea shanties for the same combination and a ballet, *Old King Cole*, for orchestra with chorus. This last was written for the Cambridge Branch of the English Folk Dance Society whose president he had become. Based on the famous nursery rhyme, it attempted to flesh the story out with a competition between the fiddlers and some explanation about why the whole event took place at all. It was performed on the lawns of Trinity College, Cambridge in the summer as part of the Cambridge Festival.

There was now more of a sense of annual routine in his life. Every year he would attend the Three Choirs Festival, where he met and exchanged ideas with other composers including Elgar and Herbert Howells, and there was the Leith Hill Festival encouraging talent from many surrounding areas, his teaching at the Royal College of Music and his direction of the Bach Choir, which began to explore further than Bach's cantatas into the more ambitious areas of his large scale works. Occasionally there was even time for a holiday, although Adeline found travel more uncomfortable with each passing year. A holiday in Venice and the Italian Mountains was marred by Adeline's illness in early 1923, but she still found the English countryside refreshing, and the couple rented a small cottage in Danbury, Essex, for the summer. Here Vaughan Williams enjoyed walking round the country lanes and settled down to compose an oratorio to be called *Sancta Civitas* (The Holy City).

Religious music was much in his thoughts at the time. Although sung in Westminster Cathedral earlier in the year, the *Mass in G Minor* had only had its first secular performance in Birmingham the previous December. Vaughan Williams had also been rehearsing the Bach choir in Bach's *St Matthew Passion* with the *St John Passion* also scheduled and their dramatic retelling of the death of Christ in solo, duet and narrative form set him thinking about

Talking to folk dancers in the 1920s.

64

such fervent religious faith. Christ's sufferings are so movingly and graphically described in the Passions that Vaughan Williams seemed to want to extend the story to its conclusion – Christ's eventual triumph – but in a visionary, more agnostic manner as though representing the universal Pilgrimage of Mankind from suffering to triumph over adversity.

He was in this frame of mind when he re-read Plato's philosophic dialogue *Phaedo*, which charts the hours before Socrates' execution on charges of corrupting the minds of the young, and this seemed to create the right mood for him to tackle basic Christian doctrines. Socrates and his pupils discuss the possibility of an afterlife. Various arguments are put forward as they debate the nature of the soul as an attunement, of its relationship to the body, the possibility of reincarnation, the nature of the Other World as stated in myths and other current ideas, before Socrates declares a measured belief in the soul's endurance after death by saying, 'Those who have cleansed themselves through philosophy exist in an incorporeal afterlife and attain even more beautiful dwelling places.' But he adds an element of doubt: 'Naturally, no thoughtful person should insist that all is as I have said, although, as we have evidence of the soul's immortality, something similar must be true. This belief is worth the risk, and I consider it reasonable, for it is a noble risk and we should be made confident by considering these accounts.'

Vaughan Williams took this last paragraph as the epigraph of *Sancta Civitas* writing it in the original Greek above the biblical texts he chose as though to reinforce his questioning agnosticism concerning a 'belief worth the risk'. Like Holst, he moved more in the direction of the visionary, extracting verses from the last book of the Bible, *The Revelations of St John the Divine*. In this apocalyptic account, the saint has a vision of the end of the world: Babylon, symbolic of all human vanity, materialism and evil, is destroyed in a great battle and Christ returns in glory to initiate 'a new heaven and a new earth' with the holy city 'coming down from heaven' in radiant splendour accompanied by a 'pure river of water of life' and the tree of life for 'the healing of the nations'. It is clear that such writing was in the same vein as Bunyan's *Pilgrim's Progress* and there are similarities between some of the music for *Sancta Civitas* and the rapt mysticism of *The Shepherds of the Delectable Mountains*; however, Vaughan Williams produces some terrifyingly dramatic music on the way as well as a moving lament for Babylon which may have influenced William Walton's similar episode in his later oratorio, *Belshazzar's Feast*. Vaughan Williams's work is a less theatrical, more private work than Walton's was going to be but in it we can discern a new direction in his output.

As he was writing *Sancta Civitas*, he heard that his opera *Hugh the Drover* was to be performed in July the following year as part of the planned Empire Exhibition. There were to be performances at the Royal College of Music first which Queen Mary would attend, followed by a professional performance given by the British National Opera Company under Malcolm Sargent in His Majesty's Theatre, London. At last, it seemed that opera by native composers was being taken seriously in England. 1923 had seen the first performances of Holst's comic opera *The Perfect Fool* at Covent Garden – although it had bemused many with its strange plot and schoolboy humour – and his chamber opera, *Savitri* had also been given at Covent Garden, where it was recognised as a masterpiece. The less substantial, more sentimental *Immortal Hour* by Rutland Boughton was enjoying a tremendous vogue whilst operas by the redoubtable Dame Ethel Smyth were also being produced. Given this new interest, Vaughan Williams had high hopes for his own ballad opera, despite knowing that its plot belonged to a more naive pre-war vision of the world and that its music stemmed from a style which he was fast outgrowing.

Holst had been fêted in America in 1923 in much the same way as Vaughan Williams had been the year before, and Vaughan Williams's *Mass in G minor* had been sung in Bach's church in Leipzig, so there seemed to be some hope that English music was beginning to 'travel' better than it had before the War, the two composers appearing in the vanguard of a new 'English' invasion. Each worked hard to promote the other's music. Holst introduced Vaughan Williams's works at his Whitsun Festivals and any other opportunity he could find and involved Vaughan Williams personally in the schools and colleges where he taught. Vaughan Williams performed Holst's new music at the Royal College of Music and Leith Hill Festivals. In one such concert at the end of 1923 Vaughan Williams conducted the Bach Choir in two performances of Holst's moving elegy for the friends they had lost in the War, the *Ode to Death*, once more to words by their favourite Walt Whitman. Holst was overjoyed and wrote:

1) It's what Ive been waiting for for 47½ years.
2) The performance was so full of You – even apart from the places I cribbed from you years ago.
3) Are you willing to sign a contract to conduct every first performance I get during the next 10 years or so?
4) You are teaching those people to sing!
5) Pray accept my blessing.

Vaughan Williams replied: '... what a wonderful experience it was for me & all of us learning your wonderful music – which got better & better as we went on.'

In April 1924, the Empire Exhibition was opened in the new Wembley Stadium in West London and, although sneered at for its jingoism by such jaded war veterans as the poet Siegfried Sassoon, who railed at 'patriotic parading with pygmy preciseness' and the inaugural speech by the King inhabiting 'vacant remoteness of air', even he was moved by the appearance of Elgar conducting massed choirs in Parry's *Jerusalem*. There were acres of pavilions, Indian palaces and native villages from all parts of the Empire and for the rest of the year the event proved immensely popular. The production of *Hugh the Drover* in the Parry Memorial Theatre at the Royal College of Music took place in July 1924. Unfortunately Vaughan Williams's old teacher and colleague, Stanford, did not see it as he had died less than two months before. Although the two composers had not always seen eye to eye, Stanford even saying that he thought Vaughan Williams and many of his contemporaries had gone musically 'mad' in recent years, they had great respect for each other, and when Vaughan Williams started to prepare his Bach Choir for their December concert he included several of Stanford's works as a memorial. Another sad loss that year was Cecil Sharp, who had done so much to save native English music from oblivion. Their former colleagues sensed that this was the end of the first era in the new English musical renaissance, but taking stock, it could now be seen that what Parry, Stanford, Sharp and their contemporaries had begun, their successors had developed into a flourishing national school and this was as fine a memorial to them as any more overt musical tribute could be.

Hugh the Drover was applauded by both audience and critics alike, which was just as well, for the later British National Opera Company production proved to be substandard. Malcolm Sargent 'saved it from disaster every few bars', Vaughan Williams said later, but on the whole he was pleased with the effect his work had had and it did not dampen his enthusiasm for the new opera revival, especially when he heard that the British National Opera Company were going to take *Hugh* on tour. Soon, he was seeking out ideas for a new libretto. Both he and Holst decided that Shakespeare's Falstaff plays would be ideal for the 'folk song' treatment

Back row: Vaughan Williams, Adeline, Holst; front row: Dorothy Longman, Vally Lasker, Nora Day.

and each set about producing his own libretto from different extracts, believing that a more genuinely English response to the setting of the fat knight's antics would not suffer by comparison with Verdi's and Nicolai's comic masterpieces. *Sir John in Love* was Vaughan Williams's treatment of *The Merry Wives of Windsor* and Holst used the tavern scenes from both parts of Henry IV for his own *At the Boar's Head* for which he intended using nothing but folk song. Holst's one-act opera was soon finished and scheduled for production with the British National Opera Company in 1925, but Vaughan Williams's four-act version would take at least another three years to complete.

Hugh the Drover was published, but Vaughan Williams had still not arranged this area of his life satisfactorily. His manuscripts had been haphazardly distributed throughout the publishing world ever since he had first sent them off for consideration, sometimes getting lost, as in the case of the full score of the *London Symphony* which had been sent to a German publishing house just before the war, never to be seen again. On that occasion it had to be laboriously recopied from orchestral parts before being resubmitted to an English publisher. Now, the Oxford University Press had accepted *The Shepherds of the Delectable Mountains* for publication and an offer came from Hubert Foss, the new director of its music publishing department, to oversee publication of all Vaughan Williams's future scores. This would take away the anxiety entailed through cold submission and, as Vaughan Williams found him sympathetic and ideally suited to his needs, he accepted. From then on OUP dealt with all the practical details of his publishing, with Vaughan Williams simply saying 'Ask Foss' whenever any difficulties arose and there is no doubt that this removed a great deal of pressure and worry from his life. He needed this, for, as a break from his public and teaching duties, he had gone with Adeline to spend the latter part of the summer in Oare, a village in a peaceful valley on Exmoor, Somerset, and was busily composing. *Sancta Civitas* was progressing there and *Sir John in Love*, but he was also writing a *Violin Concerto in D minor* and a piece for viola, wordless choir and orchestra to be called *Flos Campi* (Flower of the Field)

The influence of Bach may be seen in the concerto, as well as awareness of the Neo-Classical 'Back to Bach' movement fashionable then in continental Europe. The most prominent exponent of this style was probably Stravinsky who had produced a series of compositions from 1917 onwards including his *Symphonies for Wind Instruments* and an *Octet* for the same combination as well as experiments in opera. These works had begun to move away from Russian folk music, concentrating on earlier forms such as passacaglias and fugues, so achieving a detached and abstract style almost mathematical in its objectivity. Both Vaughan Williams and Holst were interested in Stravinsky. Holst had eschewed the popularity of his earlier orchestral works to produce a *Fugal Overture* and an ascetic *Fugal Concerto*. Vaughan Williams followed his example and now wrote his two outer movements in this tougher vein, although the violin in the slow middle movement seems to be a cousin of the ascending lark in its lyricism and there is a short quotation from *Hugh the Drover* in the last movement to show that he had not abandoned folk song. It is a good example of Vaughan Williams integrating his varied preoccupations, musical interests and styles in a work that is eclectic, but also satisfyingly his own. Perhaps realising that its new style might lead to charges of cold academicism, he forestalled the critics by calling the finished work *Concerto Accademico*, but this does not do justice to its accessibility.

Flos Campi also represented a new departure. Once more, Vaughan Williams found inspiration in the Authorized Version of the Bible, but this time he turned to that sensuous and erotic poem *The Song of Solomon*, laying it out in six movements, each headed by a quotation expressing the king's love for his beloved. These are not sung, but indicate moods ranging from an evocative delight in spring – 'the winter is past, the rain is over and gone, the flowers appear on the earth, the time of the singing of birds is come' – to the more frank 'I am sick with love ... return that we may look upon thee.' The role of the viola is that of the lover and the chorus reinforces the ardour of music that is passionate and tender, atonal and dissonant by turns. This represented one response to religious material. That year Vaughan Williams also became involved in a more basic project after being asked to edit a new hymn book to be called *Songs of Praise*. He accepted and brought as much formidable rigour of mind to the task as he had to *The English Hymnal* twenty years before.

Performances of Vaughan Williams's works were now given with more frequency, especially the *Sea Symphony* which was becoming more popular and the *Pastoral Symphony*, whose idiom was now being appreciated by previously sceptical audiences. It was even chosen for an international festival in Prague in 1925 which Ralph and Adeline attended. They had not been to the city since their honeymoon nearly twenty-seven years before and they found that it had changed from the oppressed administrative centre of an Austro-Hungarian province to the thriving capital of an independent Czechoslovakia, a status worthy of its history, architecture and long musical traditions. Adeline wrote to her sister: 'We have had an orgy of music and splendid weather. We go off tomorrow to Salzburg in Austria nr. mountains. Went to dinner at the British Legation, wasn't as terrific as I feared ... R's Pastoral got a very good reception ...'

In addition to these official engagements, they were able to attend a performance of Janáček's new opera *The Cunning Little Vixen*. Vaughan Williams was aware that Janáček's musical idiom, insofar as it was based on Czech national music, had something in common with his own but he appreciated the differences as well: Janáček had based his rhythms on the inflections of the Czech language as well as Czech music, and the results were

'Dr Vaughan Williams conducting his *Sea Symphony*, with which yesterday morning's programmes began.'
The Times, 1 November 1924.

69

startlingly effective, especially in this 'triumph of animalism' as it has been called. Modestly, Vaughan Williams considered this composition, rather than his own, to be the high point of the festival.

On their return, Vaughan Williams continued work on *Sancta Civitas* and *Sir John in Love* and decided that another opera could be made out of the one-act play which the Irish playwright J.M. Synge had written for Yeats's Abbey Theatre in Dublin. *Riders to the Sea* is a concise tragedy set on the West Coast of Ireland amongst the fishing people and he began to sketch music for it, taking the text almost in its entirety.

In October he went to the Queen's Hall, where Holst's latest work entitled *Choral Symphony No. 1* was given its London première. Due to overwork and the strain of his unwelcome popularity, Holst had suffered a nervous breakdown in the previous year and had retired to Thaxted to recuperate. This symphony was his response. He had worked in one long burst, without 'field days', on this setting of poems by John Keats and it contains many memorable and original moments. However, most of the audience and critics did not warm to it. Holst was now ceasing to be the nine-days' wonder of the musical world, as he retreated further into his own private experiments in an effort not to repeat himself. He was pleased that his popularity was waning, but he could not have enjoyed the letter Vaughan Williams sent him after this performance:

I feel I have to write & put down (chiefly for my own benefit) why I felt vaguely disappointed ... Not perhaps disappointed – I felt cold admiration – but did not want to get up & embrace everyone and then get drunk like I did after the [*Hymn of Jesus*]. I think it is only because it *is* a new work and I am more slowly moving than I used to be & it's got to soak in ...

I couldn't bear to think that I was going to 'drift apart' from you musically speaking. (If I do, who shall I have to crib from?) – I don't believe it is so – so I shall live in faith till I have heard it again several times & then I shall find out what a bloody fool I was not to see it all first time.

Forgive me this rigmarole – but I wanted to get it off my chest.

The two composers were finding their own personal ways forward, and each was at first mystified by the direction the other was taking, but they respected each other's need to develop. Earlier in the month Lionel Tertis had played the solo viola part in *Flos Campi*, which was dedicated to him, and Holst had attended. It was a brilliant performance, although it was Vaughan Williams's turn to be misunderstood. No-one could quite understand what he was trying to express. Holst wrote to him:

It was good to read and re-read your letter today. One of the reasons for its goodness being that it contains much that I felt but failed to get into words about 'Flos'.

The only point in which I differ from you is about the fear of drifting apart musically or in any other way. I expect it is the result of my old flair for Hindu philosophy and it is difficult to put simply.

It concerns the difference between life and death which means that , occasionally drifting is necessary to keep our stock fresh and sweet. It also means a lot more but that's enough for one go.

Of course there's another side and about this I'm absolutely in the dark. I mean the real value of either Flos, the KS ['Keats' Symphony], Beethoven's 9th or anything else ... During the last two years I have learnt that I don't know good music from bad, or rather, good from less good.

And I'm not at all sure that the KS is good at all. Just at present I believe I like it which is more than I can say about most of my things. ... But I'm not disappointed in Flos's composer, because he had not repeated himself. Therefore it is probably either an improvement or something that will lead to one. Which seems identical with your feelings about the KS.

I am now longing to apologize for all this rigmarole but I see you call your letter one and if getting all this off my chest gives you a quarter of the pleasure that your letter gave me it will have been well worth writing.

More of Vaughan Williams's compositions were performed in that season, including the *Sea Symphony*, *A London Symphony* and the first performance of the *Concerto Accademico* with the soloist for whom it was written, the mercurial and captivating young Hungarian Jelly d'Aranyi who was currently being fêted in London and breaking all hearts with her brilliant technique and blatant unconventionality. Holst did not hear this work, but wrote: 'I was very sorry to miss the violin concerto. So far I've only heard Vally [Lasker]'s account which was glowing.' The now-completed *Sancta Civitas* was scheduled for performance the following May.

But Vaughan Williams's pleasure at being so much in demand was marred by national events. The early hopes following the end of the War had petered out and the country seemed to be on the verge of revolution.

9 Honoured Master

There had been social discontent since post-War reforms promised by incoming governments had not materialised. Society had not changed, despite a brief taste of Ramsay MacDonald's Labour government in 1924 which had largely been thrown out of office by a Bolshevik scare. Class divisions ran as deeply as they had ever done. Whilst the wealth of the country was concentrated in the hands of a few and the privileges of the middle and upper classes were as entrenched as ever, unemployment was rife and the working classes generally badly paid. The Empire Exhibition had been only froth masking deeper problems and when Stanley Baldwin, the Prime Minister, called for all working men to take a cut in wages to help industry regain its pre-war eminence in the world, it was like a match to a tinder box. The unions, led by the miners, prepared for confrontation. Memories of the Russian Revolution caused another panic, and the government ordered police and ordinary 'white collar' citizens who had volunteered as 'specials' to be ready to meet an uprising.

The General Strike occurred between 3 and 12 May 1926, during which time food convoys were guarded, transport was manned by 'specials' protected by the army, police roamed the streets in armoured cars and demonstrations throughout the country were violently broken up. It was a classic class-war situation, and Vaughan Williams, remembering his schoolboy radicalism, the Fabian Socialist tracts he had read at University, William Morris, Bernard Shaw and their Utopianism, considering also that he had always voted either Radical or Labour, hardly knew how to react.

The General Strike.

Holst too, a former member of the Hammersmith Socialist Party and just as committed to the theories of social justice, could only write miserably to Vaughan Williams from his sound-proofed room at St Paul's Girls' School: 'I find that I am a hopeless half-hogger, and am prepared to sit on the fence, partly through laziness and partly through force of habit', and could only find comfort in a quasi-Hindu sense of inevitability.

It was in this undecided state of mind that Vaughan Williams prepared his visionary *Sancta Civitas* for performace. It was first sung during the General Strike in the Sheldonian Theatre, Oxford, as part of the Heather Festival of Music. Hugh Allen conducted, which was no mean feat as the oratorio exists on at least three levels – chorus and orchestra, semi-chorus and distant boys' chorus – which must be perfectly balanced to achieve the full effect. Nothing could be further removed from the grind of poverty, the hunger marches and the civil turmoil beyond Oxford than this ecstatically spiritual music with its hopes for 'the healing of the nations', and perhaps Vaughan Williams found some form of solace in this.

The revolution did not occur: the strike ended and the miners were slowly starved into submission without gaining any concessions; but it had been a salutory lesson to the precarious world that upper middle class musicians inhabited, and Vaughan Williams did not forget it as he busied himself with his task of enlarging the appreciation of English music. Ralph's sister Meggie had retired from the Leith Hill Festival but it was going from strength to strength under Lady Farrer who was appointed its new secretary, and it could now consider creating a more permanent, purpose-built venue for its performances in Dorking, but one that would also be of general use to the town. Vaughan Williams was always attempting to 'give the music back to the people', meaning the folk music he and his fellow-composers had 'middle-classed', to use Percy Grainger's telling phrase. He had often helped Holst at Morley College and he adjudicated for the London Labour Choral Union competitions. In addition, both he and Holst attempted to foster many other areas of music-making amongst the under-privileged while avoiding any sense of patronising them. Vaughan Williams knew how much he owed to the class so despised by many people from his own background and he made amends by writing music as much for everyday use as for the more rarified appreciation of specialists. Ironically, it is not generally appreciated that before the German composer Hindemith formulated his notion of *Gebrauchsmusik* or 'Music for Use', these two Englishmen were already writing music for ordinary people and ordinary occasions.

The London performance of *Sancta Civitas* was given in June by the London Symphony Orchestra and the Bach Choir, conducted by the composer. This was part of a four-day festival to mark the choir's golden jubilee, during which he also conducted them in both of Bach's Passions and the great *Mass in*

73

B Minor. After this triumphant feast of music, performances of the *Pastoral Symphony* at the Three Choirs Festival in Worcester Cathedral and later at a Promenade Concert in the Queen's Hall provided a calmer interlude. Work was still progressing on *Riders to the Sea* and *Sir John in Love,* Vaughan Williams being unperturbed by the semi-failure the previous year of Holst's 'Falstaff' opera, *At the Boar's Head* which had similarly been based on folk tunes. He also wrote *Six Studies in English Folk Song* for 'cello and piano and continued a new and fruitful period in his output by sketching the first two movements of a piano concerto for Harriet Cohen in which tough sonorities and percussive effects were used following his experiments in the *Violin Concerto* and *Sancta Civitas*.

1927 followed a now established pattern, Vaughan Williams spending a few weeks on walking holidays in the English countryside, but joining the increasingly incapacitated Adeline for the summer months. She now had R.O. Morris's niece, Honorine Williamson, in the household as her companion and helper. Vaughan Williams worked busily. He was commissioned to write a *Te Deum* for the enthronement of the Archbishop of Canterbury, continued to teach at the Royal College of Music, attended the Leith Hill and Three Choirs festivals as usual and conducted the Bach Choir in a production of Handel's Oratorio *Saul.* 1927 was the centenary of the death of William Blake, and the Blake scholar Geoffrey Keynes, who was distantly related to Vaughan Williams by marriage, suggested a scenario for a ballet based on some of Blake's startling *Illustrations to the Book of Job*. Vaughan Williams showed interest; he decided that as it was to be based on the Authorized Version of the Bible, it should include seventeenth century dances such as sarabands, galliards and pavanes, and he began sketching ideas for the music. In the autumn life in Cheyne Walk was threatened when Adeline broke her thigh and they knew that she could no longer manage the stairs in the five-storey house. She spent the winter in plaster and early in 1928 they were looking for a one-storey home in London.

In February, Vaughan Williams attended the London première of Holst's new tone poem *Egdon Heath,* an evocation of the wild moorland in Hardy's most pagan novel, *The Return of the Native,* dedicated to the memory of the author, recently deceased, whom both admired so deeply. The two had played it through during a 'field day' a few months previously and Vaughan Williams, still worried by the direction his friend's music was taking, had suggested 'less robust melody would have been more successful in impressionistic suggestion.' Now, after hearing the music and despite its indifferent performance by a Czech conductor and the general bewilderment of the audience, he revised his opinion, saying 'less clear melody would have softened and thereby impaired the bleak grandeur of its outline,' and he wrote to Holst himself: 'I've come to the conclusion that E.H. is beautiful – bless you therefore.' At last the two were beginning to understand each other's development as mature composers, so fulfilling the hopes of their early student days together.

In their search for a new home, Ralph and Adeline considered flats, but in the end it was decided that they should move out of London altogether to Dorking. This would give Adeline the fresh air she longed for and would still be within easy travelling distance of London on the electric railway. Despite this, Vaughan Williams decided that his commitment to the Bach Choir would be too demanding at such a distance, so he resigned, offering the post to Holst, who was inclined to accept, but was still suffering the after-effects of his nervous breakdown and was not up to the post's demands. The young Adrian Boult was eventually appointed to continue Vaughan Williams's work. Holst was well enough to organise his Whitsun Festival for 'Morleyites' and 'Paulinas' and that year it took place in the splendid surroundings of Canterbury Cathedral, where they performed Vaughan Williams's *Mass in G minor*. Holst wrote to Adeline: 'We were singing *His* (we mean *Our*) Mass from time to time and have discovered that He wrote it for this cathedral.'

Ralph and Adeline moved to a house close to Dorking for the summer, and then to one in Dorking itself which Vaughan Williams told Holst was 'our perfectly appalling address': Glory-dene, St Paul's Road. Here Vaughan Williams spent the winter working on *Job* and finishing the scoring of *Sir John in Love*. Arrangements were made for a performance of the opera to be given at the Royal College of Music Parry Memorial Theatre the following March, and early in the New Year the Vaughan Williamses returned to Cheyne Walk for the spring whilst they looked for a more permanent house in Dorking.

Malcolm Sargent conducted the first performances, and the infectious gaiety of the music was enjoyed by everyone present. Vaughan Williams had already considered the comparisons that might have been made, and dealt with them in his exuberant programme note:

To write yet another opera about Falstaff at this time of day may seem the height of impertinence for one appears in so doing to be entering into competition with four great men – Shakespeare, Verdi, Nicolai and Holst.

With regard to Shakespeare, my only excuse is that he is fair game, like the Bible, and may be made use of nowadays even for advertisements of soap and razors. I hope that it may be possible to consider that even Verdi's masterpiece does not exhaust all the possibilities of Shake-speare's genius.

And I hope that I have treated Holst with the sincerest flattery not only imitating his choice of Falstaff as the subject of an opera but in imitating his use of English folk tunes in the texture of the music. The best I can hope will be that *Sir John in Love* may be considered as a sequel to his brilliant *Boar's Head*. There remains Nicolai's *Merry Wives* which in my opinion is the most successful of all Falstaff operas; my excuse in this case is that there is hardly any Shakespeare in his libretto.

... In the matter of folk tunes, they only appear occasionally ... When a particular folk tune appeared to me the fitting accompaniment to a situation, I have used it. When I could not find a suitable folk tune, I have made shift to make up something of my own. I therefore make no apology for the occasional use of folk songs to enhance the dramatic point. If the result is successful I feel justified; if not, no amount of 'originality' will save the situation. However, the point is a small one since out of a total of 120 minutes music, the folk tunes occupy less than 15.

The text is taken almost entirely from the *Merry Wives,* with the addition of lyrics from Elizabethan poets ...

Although the production was a success, it was only an amateur one in the context of London opera, which has always been delicate when dealing with the English product, preferring to echo Alfred Einstein's opinion that 'to us Germans, English opera is inconceivable'. The earlier years of the decade had created an interest in national (or, more specifically, anti-German) opera which seemed to promise great things, but money to support it had grown more scarce with increasing economic and political uncertainty in the country. With a new Labour Government returned to office, no-one was willing to risk costly ventures, whilst impresarios, Covent Garden and even the British National Opera Company, which had supported *Hugh the Drover,* had become more cautious again. As Vaughan Williams wrote shortly afterwards, 'British opera is at present very naturally suspect.' The result was that *Sir John in Love* had to wait another seventeen years for a professional performance.

In the summer Ralph and Adeline finally located the house where they would spend the rest of their married life: 'White Gates' in Westcott Road, Dorking and it was arranged that Honorine would come to live with them to help Adeline and act as unofficial driver should they need to use a car. To the casual eye this rambling semi-bungalow with its mock-Tudor eves was no different from thousands of other suburban houses that had invaded the country-

At The White Gates,
Dorking in 1930.

With Foxy, his favourite cat.

Haymaking in the field below the White Gates. Industry has crept into the landscape.

side since the end of the war and would continue to creep ever further outward through the following decade, swallowing up the landscape and swamping whole towns and communities in a relentless flow of speculation. It might seem a strange place for a composer whose music was so deeply rooted in rural life, but Dorking, although an unremarkable town in many ways, still had good views over the surrounding countryside and Leith Hill with its curious tower in particular. Samuel Palmer had spent his last years in the uninspiring town of Redhill nearby. An artist's life is, after all, ideally one of the mind, not of his surroundings.

The house had the almost obligatory tennis court and small orchard at the back which overlooked the local parish church. There were still some fields in between and, although these were largely enclosed by the town's suburbs including a gasometer and light industry, Vaughan Williams and friends were eventually to enjoy hay-making there with long scythes, using the hay as fodder for a local horse when he started tentatively to ride again. It was quieter than Cheyne Walk, which had become a playground for 'Bright Young Things' in their noisy automobiles vying with an increasing diversity of petrol-driven vehicles of all sorts. Above all, the interior was more convenient for Adeline, with rooms entered from the large main room and its gallery above. There were window seats to catch the sun and there was space for Ralph to have his own study, which he soon cluttered up with piles of books and manuscript paper. And the cats liked it. He was also closer to the Leith Hill Festival and he could devote more time to its expansion. That year alone he had signalled his ambitions by including Purcell's *King Arthur* and Haydn's *The Seasons* in the

programmes and, knowing that the following year it was celebrating its Silver Jubilee, he had a great deal of preparation in prospect.

He wrote three works especially for the festival that year. The most expansive was the *Benedicite* for mixed Soprano, Chorus and Orchestra, taking the words of the Canticle beginning 'O all ye works of the Lord: bless ye the Lord' and adding the 'Song of the Three Holy Children' by the seventeenth-century poet J. Austin. He also finished *Job* which he called 'a masque for dancing' rather than a ballet. He had modified Keynes's original scenario to nine scenes with an introduction and epilogue. In each, Satan's trial of Job is portrayed through the death of his sons and daughters-in-law, the loss of his wealth, the taunting of the 'comforters' represented by an oily saxophone, his final rejection of God, the fall of Satan and the return of Job to God's favour. This theme of suffering transmuted into redemption and wisdom is in a direct line from other post-war works by Vaughan Williams including *The Shepherds of the Delectable Mountains* and *Sancta Civitas* and the music seemed to be summing up many of his styles, veering from stylised pastoral sarabands and folk themes to the harshest of dissonances in the matter of a few bars. In so doing, he captured both the terror and innocence – that 'inner eye' – of Blake's biblical vision whose mystical dimension could see angels on the hills of London and sensed the deepest essence of man's mind in the notion of Albion. To Blake, the twin poles of God and Satan represented warring areas of the human psyche and Vaughan Williams responded with music that mirrors this ambiguity, the appeal of this dramatic opposition lying in what Blake had said of Milton, that 'he was of the Devil's party but did not know it.' Needless to say, such an English theme did not interest the urbane Diaghilev when it was offered to him for his *Ballets Russes*, and Vaughan Williams was not too unhappy with this as he remarked later, 'I feel that the Russian Ballet would have made an unholy mess of it with their over-developed calves.' Instead, a concert performance was scheduled for the Norwich Festival of October 1930.

In complete contrast to the turbulent and visionary music of *Job* and the harrowing plot of *Riders to the Sea* on which he was still working, Vaughan Williams decided to write an operetta in the style made fashionable by Gilbert and Sullivan and Edward German, but also with more than a passing nod to the witty, satirical revues of Noel Coward and others who were so much in vogue during the twenties and early thirties. The story he chose was *The Poisoned Kiss* by Richard Garnett, adapted into a libretto by Evelyn Sharp. Its improbable premise is that a young woman has been nurtured with poison from birth in order to kill any young man who might be interested in her. The idea was to aim satirical darts at the foppish 'Young Things', the world of advertising, and any other area of contemporary life that the librettist thought ripe for mockery, and Vaughan Williams set about writing

78

the music to this 'romantic extravaganza' with gusto.

Living out of London did not mean that Vaughan Williams could vegetate or grow isolated: friends came down to stay with the couple in Dorking and he still visited the capital regularly to teach and attend concerts, including a rare week-long Delius Festival arranged by the composer's champion, Thomas Beecham. As Adeline wrote, 'I see it is best to live amongst the cabbages and have an orgy now and then.' 1930 was to be a busy year. He was presented with the Royal Philharmonic Society's Gold Medal in March and attended the same event a month later to see the medal awarded to Holst after a concert that included the latter's neo-classical *Double Violin Concerto*. Although Holst, who refused and hated nearly all honours, was too busy trying to escape from the congratulations of officials to see Vaughan Williams, and was later photographed scowling at the medal, Vaughan Williams wrote to him the next day with a typically frank criticism of his new composition:

I was distressed not to see you last night, I know you hate it all – but we had to tell you in public that we know you are a great man.

The Lament and Ground are splendid – I'm not *quite* so sure about the scherzo – and even that boils down to not being *quite* sure about the 6/8 tune.

The Jubilee Leith Hill Festival was a gratifying success despite the Dorking Halls not being finished in time. The *Benedicite,* a work in Vaughan Williams's most public and festive vein, provided the right atmosphere of rejoicing and he was effusively thanked for his contributions over the years from the very inception of the annual event, during which time he had cajoled, raged, let loose his boisterous humour and finally charmed his choirs and orchestras into performances of such high standards. Malcolm Sargent conducted another performance of *Sir John in Love* in Oxford that May which Ralph and Adeline attended and where they also met Holst; then in July the University of Wales, mindful of Vaughan Williams's Welsh ancestry, made him an honorary Doctor of Music. In October, the couple joined Holst and Ralph's elderly mother in Norwich for the first performance of *Job* in its concert version. Holst had helped Vaughan Williams with the score from its inception and the latter subsequently wrote:

I should like to place on record all that he did for me when I wrote *Job*. I should be alarmed to say how many 'Field Days' we spent over it. Then he came to all the orchestral rehearsals, including a special journey to Norwich.

The work was preceded by Janáček's exuberantly impressive *Glagolitic Mass* which seems to have stolen some of its thunder, and critics were 'less than lukewarm' and a little unsure about the new direction Vaughan Williams seemed to be taking. Even so the music of *Job* did not fail to impress and shortly afterwards

Holst persuaded the celebrated ballerina Ninette de Valois to stage the work the following year in London for her Camargo Society (the forerunner of Sadler's Wells Ballet).

After spending what Adeline called 'a most delightful and exciting London season' during which they attended a performance of the *Sea Symphony* conducted by Adrian Boult, and Vaughan Williams heard Holst's *The Planets*, Ralph and Adeline returned to Dorking for the winter, although Ralph continued to visit London regularly and on one memorable occasion visited Holst at St Paul's School to hear a run-through of three of his friend's new works in the sound-proof room. The *Choral Fantasia* for chorus, organ and orchestra, his one-act opera *The Wandering Scholar* and a Prelude and Scherzo for wind band entitled *Hammersmith* in which Holst paid tribute to the river and area of London he knew so well, were all performed in reduced piano versions. Vaughan Williams wrote:

The Organ Concerto [*Choral Fantasia*] is *IT* all right ... the opera gave me quite a new idea – the *concert opera*: sit round a table *with copies* and sing with a minimum of action (*no costumes*). I thought it was a perfect representation ... The one thing I can't yet quite get hold of is 'Hammersmith' – but you are (like your daughter) a realist & you are almost unique in that your stuff sounds better when it is played on the instrument it was originally written for.

I want very much to have a lesson on 'Riders' [to the Sea] soon. I've been revising and rough scoring it.

In addition to working on *Riders to the Sea* Vaughan Williams had now finished his *Piano Concerto* with a monumental fugal finale. He was also sketching a new symphony which promised to be equally uncompromising in idiom and on which he spent several 'field days' working with Holst. He had ambitious plans for the Leith Hill Festival, intending to perform Bach's *St Matthew Passion* to celebrate the opening of the Dorking Halls the following March. Vaughan Williams had very definite views on the performance of Bach which he later encapsulated in a radio talk and essay entitled 'Bach the Great Bourgeois'. For him there should be no return to 'authenticity' with the music 'performed as "period music" in the precise periwig style' for he believed that Bach would have relished the improvements in instruments that had developed since his day. 'Would he not have been thrilled and uplifted' by the sound? Vaughan Williams asked, and he imagined Bach saying, 'this is not what I ever hoped to hear, but it realises and more than realises what was in my mind.' Vaughan Williams's performances were played on modern instruments and sung in English with a piano continuo, for he said:

The harpsichord, however it may sound in a small room – and to my mind it never has a pleasant sound – in a large concert room sounds just like the ticking of a sewing machine. We have no longer, thank Heaven, the Baroque style of organ [so] we cannot perform Bach exactly as he was played in his time even if we wanted to, and the question is, do we want to? I say emphatically, 'No!' ... Why should we perform Bach with all the disabilities under which he suffered any more than we perform Shakespeare in the Elizabethan pronunciation? If by modifying the letter we kill the spirit of Bach, then he had better remain dead and be put in the museum with the other mummies. Through all the changes and chances, the beauty of his music abides because his music appeals to everyone – not only to the aesthete, the musicologist or the propagandist, but above all to Whitman's 'Divine Average' – the great middle class from whom nearly all that is worth while in religion, painting, poetry and music is sprung.

In the end, the performance turned out to be a memorial concert, for Vaughan Williams's sister Meggie died in January. She had worked tirelessly to establish the festival and had made its maintenance her life's work. Unfortunately, she had not had a happy life, becoming slightly eccentric towards the end, but her brother produced a fitting tribute to her with Bach's masterpiece moving many of the audience to tears.

Despairing of getting *Sir John in Love* into the repertoire, Vaughan Williams arranged some of the most immediately attractive music into a cantata – *In Windsor Forest*. In early summer, Honorine drove Ralph and Adeline down to Chichester where Holst's friend Bishop Bell had made the cathedral available for his Whitsun Festival, but Vaughan Williams was able to attend rehearsals for *Job* in London afterwards. They progressed with difficulty, the 'Englishness' of the conception seeming to elude Ninette de Valois at first, although Adeline was able to report that there was 'a very nice God on his throne' and later, 'the scenery looked beautiful – such a noble flock of painted sheep and Mrs Job was a joy.' When it had seemed that no-one was willing to stage *Job*, Vaughan Williams had scored it for a large orchestra but it was essential to reduce this for the theatre and so a new arrangement was entrusted to Constant Lambert. The performances in July at the Cambridge Theatre in London and later in Oxford seem to have done justice to a difficult concept, with a magnificent green Satan stealing the show. Vaughan Williams was generally pleased with the effect, especially when the ballet company included the work in its repertory and regularly went on tour with it. Vaughan Williams said later 'I owe the life of *Job* to Holst' and wrote to him after the production: 'I never wrote to thank you for holding my hand all those days – it made all the difference. All went very well in the end.'

The Three Choirs Festival was held in Gloucester that year, and Vaughan Williams was able to attend the first performance of Holst's *Choral Fantasia*. Bernard Shaw was in the audience as usual and was one of the critics who dismissed the work roundly, but Vaughan Williams rallied to his friend's defence, writing to him: 'I played through the fantasia again yesterday & it is *most* beautiful – I know you don't care, but I just want to tell the press ... that they are misbegotten abortions.'

Shortly afterwards Vaughan Williams accepted an invitation to conduct a choir of Welsh miners in Wales. They performed *Toward the Unknown Region* and Vaughan Williams was greatly moved by the singing and the way the local people were struggling against their deprived conditions by reclaiming virtual slag heaps for allotments to feed their families. The new decade had begun grimly with mass unemployment increasing and political movements of both the extreme Right and Left capitalising on the discontent and, once more, Vaughan Williams felt uneasily that a man with his advantages should do as much as possible to achieve a balance between his own Establishment position and that of the less fortunate in society. Consequently, the knighthoods that Stanford, Parry, Elgar and many other of his contemporaries accepted were not his style, and the only honours he would accept were musical or academic ones, preferring to be styled, 'plain "Mr", or, if you prefer, "Dr" Vaughan Williams.' He was thus willing to collect the honorary Doctor of Laws conferred on him in December at Liverpool University on his merits alone.

He received an invitation early in 1932 to return to America and lecture at Bryn Mawr College in Pennsylvania for the autumn

82

term. He accepted and in March wrote to Holst, who was at the time on a lecturing and conducting tour of America:

... I'm longing for news ... I miss you very much when I want to know how to compose – in [fact] I didn't realise how much you wrote of my music before.

I wonder how you enjoy being led by the nose by an American agent – an agent ... wrote to me and wanted to lead me round America for several months – but I shied off.

... I do want to know how America goes – & *have you time for your own work* – because I believe the change will produce a great new work from you. But perhaps that will come when you get back – 'emotion remembered in tranquillity' etc.

Did I tell you that I am writing a 'Magnificat' for Worcester Fest[ival]? The story is as follows:

(a) ... I wondered if it wd be possible to lift the words out of the smug atmosphere which has settled down on it from being sung at evening service for so long. (I've tried hard to get the smugness out; I don't know if I have succeeded – I find it awfully hard to eradicate it.)

(b) Last year at Gloucester rehearsals Steuart [Wilson] (I think) said that it was not quite nice that young unmarried women like Elsie Suddaby should always be singing Magnificats – so Astra Desmond who was there said to me 'I'm a married woman with 4 children why don't you write one for me' – So I promised her if ever I wrote one it should be for her.

Come back soon.

Holst replied from Harvard University:

It's grand news about the Magnificat and I hope to see it soon. Steuart's theology sounds a little unorthodox but his commonsense is unquestionable.

How's the new Sym? [No.4] When I get home in July I want a 2 piano field day of both old and new versions. When do you arrive in the USA? How long will you stay? And will you be able to visit Harvard? In that case I'll lend you Davison's front door key ... It's a useful thing to have in this country.

I'm very glad I've made use of Duncan McKenzie (OUP) as an agent. He has been really helpful and I hope you'll at least consider using him. The alternative would be to print 1000 forms –

'Dear Sir or Madame
    I'll be damned before I'll conduct, lecture, dine, be interviewed, be photographed' –

I forget the others but there are a few left. You'd probably have to accept all the Mus Docs – I've just refused the 2nd in a month.

Holst then gave Vaughan Williams the first intimations that he was seriously ill:

On Easter Day, after lecturing on Haydn in Washington the previous day and having a horrid 14 hour journey back at night, they took me to hospital with a duodenal ulcer. And I learnt the real meaning of the phrase 'A Bloody Nuisance'. They reckoned that I lost two quarts. They gave me a) blood transfusion which was invigorating at first but which gave me a high temperature the next day: b) morphia which is altogether delightful: c) five days diet of 'creamed milk' every hour which was infernal.

I had one beautiful experience which was repeated two nights later. I felt I was sinking so low that I couldn't go much further and remain on earth. As I have always expected, it was a lovely feeling although the second time, as it began, I had a vague feeling that I ought to be thinking of my sins. But a much stronger feeling was that there was something more important on hand and that I mustn't waste time. Both times, as soon as I reached the bottom I had one clear, intense and calm feeling – that of overwhelming Gratitude. And the four chief reasons for gratitude were Music, the Cotswolds, RVW and having known the impersonality of orchestral playing.

I was in hospital 16 days and since then have been staying with the Davisons who are dears. Every day I've been getting stronger and walking more . . .

My movements are uncertain. If the doctor allows I go to conduct at Ann Arbor about May 17 and then on to Vancouver Island after which a holiday in the Rockies and then home.

But I'm not running any risks and if all these nights and meals in trains won't do I'll come back in the middle of June.

Love to Adeline.

Get on with the Symphony.

Due to his illness, Holst returned to England earlier than he had anticipated, but by September he felt sufficiently recovered to visit Ralph and Adeline's home where he worked with Ralph on his new symphony. After his three previous symphonies which had all been in some ways programmatic, this was to be simply labelled 'Symphony in F minor' and was becoming a toughly argued exercise in pure symphonic music with outbursts of savage dissonance. Despite the ominous political troubles on the continent from which Britain was in no way immune, Vaughan Williams later denied that it was in any way prophetic of future conflict, stating, 'I wrote it not as a definite picture of anything external – e.g. the state of Europe – but simply because it occurred to me like this ... It is what I wanted to do *at the time*,' and some commentators have considered it to be a self-portrait, even linking it to Beethoven's Fifth symphony in its power and complete lack of compromise. Vaughan Williams was very grateful to Holst for his help in shaping the music and wrote to him after one of their 'field days':

It was wonderful having you on Tues: I feel ashamed of myself sometimes letting you waste all that nervous energy which you ought to be spending on your own stuff for me – But it's too late to mend now & I can't get on without you, so that's that ... I wish we had more talk about you & what really matters & not spent so much time over my damned compos.

That same month, the two composers were in Worcester for the Three Choirs Festival where Vaughan Williams's new *Magnificat* was performed together with Holst's *Hymn of Jesus*. In his attempt to remove any sense of 'smugness', Vaughan Williams had written the *Magnificat*, not from the point of view of the angel who informs Mary that she is to become the Mother of God, but from Mary's point of view as a tender response of a girl to her lover, the Holy Spirit, which is represented by a solo flute. In this way, he produced a human version of a mystical religious prayer, in complete contrast to the symphony he was struggling to write.

This time, Adeline was not well enough to accompany Ralph on the long crossing to America in the autumn. Before heading for Pennsylvania, he took a short break, staying with Holst's friend, the musicologist Archibald Davison, and his wife. He wrote to Holst:

I had a splendid 2 days with the Davisons – they were both so nice – and while in Boston I went to i) a football match and ii) Boston Symph. Orch.; both suffer I think from being too much organised. Tonight I shall hear Phila. Orch. and on Monday N.Y. Orch.

I am feeling very happy here and everyone is v. hospitable – I went to a music store in Phila[delphia] yesterday and was introduced to the Manager – it was just like a chapter out of Martin Chuzzlewit.

His lectures on National Music were well received and afterwards he had time to visit the theatre in Philadelphia where he saw Holst's brother Emil performing in a play which greatly amused him. His two-month trip ended in New York which he called 'more classically and tragically beautiful than ever' when the skyscrapers lit up after sunset, but he was glad when the tour was over and he could return to Dorking.

He spent the winter working on the symphony and *Riders to the Sea* which he had also discussed with Holst. Holst had a relapse

A 'prom' in the Queen's Hall.

after Christmas, although he was able to send Vaughan Williams six canons he had written for unaccompanied voices. Vaughan Williams wrote to him, 'For our sake you must keep well – but for the sake of music you must go on writing canons – so try and continue the two.' Unfortunately Holst did not recover quickly and had to enter a nursing home in January. This made it impossible for him to attend the first performance of Vaughan Williams's *Piano Concerto* at the beginning of February 1933. It was given in the Queen's Hall with its dedicatee, Harriet Cohen, as soloist and the BBC Symphony Orchestra conducted by Adrian Boult. Vaughan Williams admitted that he had been inspired by Busoni's music, especially his transcriptions of Bach, and the generally massive sound that Vaughan Williams produced might in some ways have been an emulation of Busoni's elephantine piano concerto. The work impressed many critics who had previously considered Vaughan Williams nothing more than an eccentric folk song composer of the 'cow pat' school, but shortly afterwards Adrian Boult suggested that the soloist's role was too demanding and the work might lie better if arranged for two pianos and orchestra. Vaughan Williams agreed and asked Holst's opinion on this and other revisions when he had recovered later in the year. Holst replied. 'Thanks for letter re the concerto. I can quite believe that the slow pace for the fugue would make a big difference. How I wish I could have heard it.' In the end he asked Joseph Cooper to help him rearrange the work, but other considerations delayed this new version.

There were minor irritations to deal with that summer. Vaughan Williams fell into a ditch and broke his leg, so was bedridden for some time before hobbling round on crutches. The house in Dorking was also full of builders who were enlarging it with a view to eventually accommodating Vaughan Williams's ageing mother, so he and Adeline escaped to Eastbourne where Ralph recuperated. He was well enough to conduct a performance of the *Pastoral Symphony* at the Promenade Concert at the end of August. Holst had recovered sufficiently to attend and wrote to Vaughan Williams:

It is difficult to thank you for last night because I've said it all before. I went expecting a real treat but I doubt if I've ever been so carried away by it before – which is saying a great deal.

And I'm going to repeat myself – it's the very essence of you.

Which is one of the two reasons (the other being that it is a beautiful work of art) why it is such an important event in my life.

Vaughan Williams continued to revise the F minor symphony, which Holst still took an interest in despite his health having deteriorated to such an extent that he was confined to another nursing home in December. It was hoped that six weeks of restricted diet and rest would cure him there and Vaughan Williams wrote to him:

I was so glad of your letter – it is largely good news – but 6 weeks! I must certainly come and see you if it is allowed.

The 'nice' tunes in the Finale [of the F minor Symphony] have already been replaced with better ones (at all events they are *real* ones). What I mean is that I *knew* the others were made-up stuff and these are not. So there we are. . .

The cure did not work, and Holst was told that his only hope of full recovery would be to undergo a major operation. He agreed and surgery was scheduled for May. Whilst he prepared himself, news came at the end of February of the death of the most respected of all English composers, Elgar. Although he had been virtually silent since the end of the war, he was still considered the doyen of English composers, still held the post of Master of the King's Music and was a familiar figure at the Three Choirs Festival where both Vaughan Williams and Holst knew him well, so that his death left a vacuum in English music that would not be easily filled. In a tribute to him Vaughan Williams conducted a performance of *The Dream of Gerontius* at the Leith Hill Festival that year.

Whilst Holst was in hospital, Vaughan Williams helped by

taking some of his lessons at St Paul's and continued to correspond with him. He listened to performances of his music on the wireless, writing, 'Tomorrow is Tertis and your viola piece [*Lyric Movement* for Viola and Small Orchestra] – I hope my wireless will not go wrong,' and again, after a performance of his *Choral Symphony* had been broadcast in April, he wrote

After promising myself all the year that I would attend *every* rehearsal of the choral symphony I attended *none* – I stupidly went in for a little chill & temperature – nothing bad, but ... I thought I must take no risks. I was never so disgusted in my life. [Our] wireless behaved pretty well – funnily the scherzo came over best, I thought ... & it *was* a relief to hear the [Ode on a Grecian] Urn [the slow movement] sung by people who had some idea what the words meant ...

As to the tune itself – I *wholly* liked the Urn for the first time. I'm not sure that it is the Urn – but it's *you*, which is all I know & all I need to know.

The scherzo is what I always thought it was; you at your best.

I am not so sure about the finale. I love the big tune, but some of it seems to be just getting through the words. I wonder if a cut of one or two of the poems would be possible or advisable?

With this letter, Vaughan Williams reconciled himself to the work that had created earlier misunderstandings between the two friends. It was a final gesture of reconciliation, but Holst had no time to take his friend's well-meant advice for on 25 May he died, two days after the operation that he had hoped would give him a new lease of life. It was the end of one of the most profound and mutually supportive of all musical friendships, and Vaughan Williams was deeply affected by the loss.

10 A Low Dishonest Decade

My only thought is now which ever way I turn, what are we to do without him – everything seems to have turned back to him – what would Gustav think or advise or do –

So Vaughan Williams wrote to Holst's wife and daughter after the service for the interment of his ashes in Chichester Cathedral. They were buried close to the memorial of Thomas Weelkes, as singers from Morley College and St Paul's performed the 'Kyrie' from Vaughan Williams's *Mass in G minor*, an anthem by Weelkes and Holst's own joyous 'Tomorrow shall be my dancing day' which inspired *The Hymn of Jesus*. A few days later, Adrian Boult conducted a memorial concert on the wireless which included Holst's *Ode to Death*, his *Dirge for Two Veterans* and *Egdon Heath*.

Vaughan Williams had many friends and a devoted, intelligent and musical wife. He was respected as much as any of his contemporaries, who included his friend the symphonist Arnold Bax and the new Master of the King's Music, Walford Davies, and was admired by younger British composers, including Arthur Bliss and William Walton; but, now that his greatest friend and helper had gone and after the death of Delius was announced in June, he seemed an increasingly isolated figure. He was sixty-one and more than ever gave the impression of being representative of an earlier generation, with his presidencies of English folk music societies and his occasional arrangements of folk tunes – that year for a typically English pageant play. His appearance, gruffly eccentric at the best of times, also seemed to have more *gravitas* than usual. He had once more had to spend a long period in bed after poisoning the leg he had earlier broken and, when he could at last appear in public, he was supported by a walking stick. In this manner, he conducted the *London Symphony* and a new arrangement of folk tunes, *The Running Set* at a Promenade Concert in the autumn and, when helped off the platform, was applauded like the Grand Old Man of music. Yet it was not that long since he had surprised everyone with *Job* and the brutally percussive *Piano Concerto*, and he was just finishing the symphony that would set loose more shocks in the musical world, making him seem more like the Angry Young Man of Music.

During his incapacity, he had observed the darkening political situation in Italy and Germany, where Fascists and Nazis had come to power and were sabre-rattling with much racist and xeno-phobic rant. He wrote, 'I wonder what is going to happen – this looks like the break up of everything with Mussolini thundering at the door.' In London, Oswald Mosley's Blackshirts were taunting Jews in the East End whilst intellectuals led by Shaw and H.G. Wells urged the younger generation of thinkers to support the Russian Communist experiment. With the Depression taking hold in America and Britain, hunger marchers descending on London from the deprived provincial regions, and the fear of revolt that might follow, it seemed as though everything Vaughan Williams and his generation had fought for and believed in was coming to an end.

It was in this atmosphere of foreboding at the beginning of 1935 that he accepted the chairmanship of a committee to build a Music Hall as a memorial to Holst at Morley College – to be sound-proofed and decorated with a fresco of the planets – and also helped organise memorial concerts for his friend. The new symphony went into rehearsal under Adrian Boult shortly afterwards. This was like an unspoken memorial, for Holst had helped shape it more than anyone apart from Vaughan Williams himself. It was during rehearsal discussions that Vaughan Williams remarked, 'I don't know whether I like it, but it's what I meant' and the first performance stunned even those critics and musicians who had heard the rumour that something extraordinarily powerful was coming from his pen.

As part of his Silver Jubilee celebrations that year, the King awarded Vaughan Williams the Order of Merit – an exclusive gift from the Sovereign which he accepted for what it was, a recognition of merit rather than an empty title. Elgar had also been a member of this exclusive order, and it was a memory of one of his suggestions that now prompted a new 'choral suite' as Vaughan Williams called it. Three years earlier, Elgar had been talking to him at the Three Choirs Festival and had told him that he had once wanted to write an oratorio based on the bibulous 'Elinor Rumming' by John Skelton, poet laureate at the time of Henry VIII and a writer as bawdy and satirical as Chaucer before him. By the time he mentioned it, he felt he was no longer up to the task and suggested that Vaughan Williams should try his hand at it. Having just finished writing his comic operetta *The Poisoned Kiss* which was about to be put into production, Vaughan Williams re-read Skelton's racy verses, choosing a selection for his *Five Tudor Portraits*. What he produced may be seen as a secular cantata in five movements dealing not only with the disreputable hag Elinor Rumming and her alehouse in Leatherhead full of drunks and gossips – a place where Falstaff and his cronies would have been at home – but the much-hated and insulted clerk John Jayberd of Diss, the dashing young rogue Jolly Rutterkin, the contrasting, bitter-sweet love poem to 'Pretty Bess' and a lament by the convent girl Jane Scroop for her pet sparrow who has been killed by a cat. Vaughan Williams said, 'Jane saw no reason, and I see no reason why she should not pray for the peace of her sparrow's soul,' and he produced a long and genuinely moving elegy for the dead bird. The whole work reflects his own interest and sympathy with the more human aspects of the Tudor period.

His own humanity continued to be touched by the news coming from Europe, where Hitler and Mussolini were re-arming their countries on a war footing and the Nazis were beginning to suppress all opposition, introducing their anti-minority policies and posturing in sinister rallies at Nuremberg. It was in this frame of mind that he turned to a commission he had received from the Huddersfield Choral Society for a work to commemorate their centenary the following year. Perhaps reminded by the performance of Holst's *Dirge for Two Veterans* played shortly after his funeral, he found his own setting of the Whitman poem which he had put aside in 1911 and decided to incorporate it into a cantata which would cry out for peace. The very title, *Dona Nobis Pacem* (Give Us Peace), leaves no doubt as to its theme, and he assembled a collection of texts including war poems by Walt Whitman, the Bible and an extract from John Bright's speech in the House of Commons during the Crimean War, beginning 'The Angel of Death has been abroad throughout the land.' This eclectic selection exactly suited his needs and combined into a unity which allowed the music to progress from anguished cries for peace, through a savage depiction of war invading every aspect of life, to a plea for reconciliation followed by the description of the funeral of the two veterans 'father and son', the Angel of Death sequence, a final hope for future peace when 'Nation shall not lift up a sword against Nation' and a vision of 'new heavens and the new earth' echoing the mystical conclusion of *Sancta Civitas* but with a closer urgency.

Sancta Civitas was the work that Vaughan Williams conducted at the Three Choirs Festival in the autumn, and it mirrored a theme of disquiet that could be sensed everywhere. The year also saw the release of an ambitious film based on H.G. Wells's *The Shape of Things to Come*. This production alone seemed to take the British cinema out of the doldrums of mass entertainment it had inhabited since the beginning of the 'talkies' and started a remarkable trend. Its apocalyptic vision of a world devastated by swaggering war lords and then redeemed by town-and-country planners whose gleaming new future incorporates space ships to the stars may have dated, but not the power of the music which the producers commissioned from Arthur Bliss. The success of his score would encourage them to spread their net wider over the years, taking in other 'serious' composers including Vaughan Williams.

George V died in January 1936 and was succeeded by his son, the dashing, but light-weight and politically ambiguous Edward VIII. Vaughan Williams wrote a short elegiac piece for the dead king, but was more interested in the performances of his F minor Symphony coupled with *Job* which was one of the few concerts arranged by the British Council for visiting foreign critics. With Italy now pursuing imperial ambitions by invading Abyssinia, and music by 'decadent' composers being proscribed in totalitarian states where bonfires of 'non-Aryan' books and music were already lighting the skies, it seemed that all such international contacts might soon dry up.

An antidote to such gloomy ideas was provided by the première of *The Poisoned Kiss* at Cambridge and later at Sadler's Wells, London. Although written in Vaughan Williams's most cheerful and exuberant vein, it did not seem to hit the mark, falling, like Holst's comic opera, *The Perfect Fool* under the imbalance of its silly libretto. The *Five Tudor Portraits* were also first performed that year, in September during the Norwich Festival, sharing the programme with the première of *Our Hunting Fathers*, an astringent work by the young Benjamin Britten using the political poems of W.H. Auden as a response to the European situation. Vaughan Williams's work was vastly enjoyed, despite upsetting one elderly countess in the audience, but his cantata *Dona Nobis Pacem*, premièred at the Huddersfield Choral Society's centenary in October, sent shock waves of compassion and fear through the audience. It also reached a wider audience over the airwaves of the BBC and, placed amongst the news bulletins of the Abyssinian and Spanish Civil wars, must have touched the rawest of collective nerves.

It seemed that no sooner had he become King, and begun to show some social conscience by touring the coal mining communities, meeting the unemployed and announcing 'something must be done', much to the embarrassment of his ministers, than Edward VIII had abdicated to marry Mrs Simpson, an American divorcee. The British public, who had seen three kings in one year, nevertheless prepared for the usual loyal festivities surrounding the coronation of his brother, George VI, and none more so than Vaughan Williams who wrote a sonorous *Flourish* and a *Te Deum* for the event. When it took place in May 1937, the processions

At the Three Choirs Festival between Herbert Howells (left) and Rutland Boughton (right).

and appearance of so many representatives of the Empire created a public relations exercise on a scale unparalleled since the crowning of George V and must have contrasted strongly with the general mood of the nation, although they gave it a focus for national pride and confidence in its own appearance of greatness. It is not without irony that just such a coronation shortly preceded the outbreak of the First World War.

As a member of the Order of Merit, Vaughan Williams was invited to the most important ceremonies, including the coronation itself and the Portsmouth naval review that followed. Once more a parade of naval might was used both for ceremonial and political reasons although Vaughan Williams, with his great capacity for enjoyment, relished every colourful and spectacular moment. *Dona Nobis Pacem* was performed at the Leeds Festival and Three Choirs Festival in Gloucester that year, and this made the offer of an unusual award from Hamburg University a problem. Its Shakespeare Prize was conferred for any one of a whole range of the arts, and Vaughan Williams thought it might make English music better known in Germany if he accepted, but he did not want to compromise his ideals. He wrote:

... I am strongly opposed to the present system of government in Germany, especially with regard to its treatment of artists and scholars. I belong to more than one English society whose object is to combat all that the present German *régime* stands for. Therefore am I the kind of person to whom a German University would wish to offer a prize?

He was assured that the prize was purely for merit and not a propaganda ploy, so he accepted the invitation to receive it in person in Hamburg the following year.

Shortly afterwards, Vaughan Williams's mother died, aged ninety-five. He had always loved and respected her, realising that she represented everything that was tough and uncompromising in his own makeup and everything that was open-minded and fair in his background. This left his brother Hervey, now a childless widower, in sole possession of Leith Hill Place, and Ralph was troubled by the thought that he might eventually inherit it himself.

At last *Riders to the Sea*, the opera he had worked on for seven years, was performed in December. Malcolm Sargent conducted at the Royal College of Music and many realised that this was Vaughan Williams's most perfect attempt in the medium so far, despite its brevity. Forty minutes of closely-woven music set the atmospheric background to the Irish fishing community where the action takes place, and his use of a recitative style to mirror the speech-rhythms of the protagonists was a new departure for him. He had chosen to use virtually the entire text of Synge's play concerning the deaths of the male members of a family, all taken by the sea, and the tragic nobility of the surviving mother who blesses them in a final prayer as the sea keens in the distance, the music hinting at later works that were to explore this theme of nobility in the face of adversity.

Just when the world seemed to be turning towards a new barbarism, Vaughan Williams began another symphony, this time in D major, not in the harsh, uncompromising style of his earlier 'warning' works, but one that seemed to breathe the same air as the *Pastoral*. This earlier symphony had been his own personal attempt to come to terms with the mass destruction and death he had witnessed on the Western Front, and now it was almost as though he saw in the ideals of Bunyan and his visionary city of eternal light a beacon that might yet 'heal the nations'. Music that he had written for *The Shepherds of the Delectable Mountains* seemed to be the starting point for this *Symphony in D*, which also paraphrases other music that Vaughan Williams had written for sections of *The Pilgrim's Progress* although the work would take at least another five years to complete.

1938 saw the *Anschluß* – Hitler's enforced union of Germany and Austria and shortly afterwards the dictator began demanding the Sudetenland, a German-speaking part of Czechoslovakia. Vaughan Williams conducted *Dona Nobis Pacem* twice that year, once at the Leith Hill Festival and later at the Three Choirs Festival in response to these events, but he did go to Hamburg in June to receive the Shakespeare Prize, making a plea in his acceptance speech for a greater appreciation of English music in Germany and a hope that this would strengthen understanding between the two peoples. The *London Symphony* and the *Tallis Fantasia* were performed to reinforce this, and, although he was aware of the trappings of Nazism all around, Vaughan Williams knew he was also in Brahms's city and visited his birthplace and Bach's city of Lübeck nearby. It was this civilised aspect of the Germans that truly mattered to him, not the ubiquitous swastikas and Nazi salutes.

Shakespeare now provided the inspiration for a commission that was dear to his heart. Sir Henry Wood was celebrating his Golden Jubilee in October that year and Vaughan Williams was asked to write a work for sixteen of the conductor's favourite singers so that they might perform it at a concert scheduled to mark the event. He chose a speech from *The Merchant of Venice* in praise of music, containing the words:

> The man that hath no music in himself,
> Nor is not moved with concord of sweet sounds,
> Is fit for treasons, stratagems and spoils.

Scored for sixteen soloists and orchestra, the *Serenade to Music* is written in his most serene vein. Dedicated to Sir Henry Wood 'in grateful recognition of his services to music', it formed the centrepiece of the concert and was recorded shortly afterwards by the same forces, although Vaughan Williams also made arrangements for chorus, and for a reduced number of soloists so that one of his warmest and most gratifying works could be performed more frequently.

Vaughan Williams had now given up his teaching at the Royal College of Music to concentrate more on music-making, but he was still active on committees agitating on behalf of musicians and composed a large amount of 'music for use'. The Anglican Services he wrote for Christ's Hospital and a pageant for the Dorking and Leith Hill District Preservation Society fell into this category. He collaborated with the novelist E.M. Forster, directing and collating music for the ironically titled *England's Pleasant Land*. This satirised the decade's explosion of suburbia with its identical 'cottage style' houses stretching for miles and selling for as little as £400 a time. But they were preaching to the deaf, for those people whose prosperity had increased following the Depression dreamt of buying just such a house, with a garage attached for a mass-produced Model T Ford.

He was also making sketches for an entertainment variously described as a mime, ballet or masque entitled *Epithalamion*, based on the writings of the Elizabethan poet Edmund Spenser, and submitted to him by Ursula Wood, a young admirer who was to become a confidante and friend. He was also working on a commission for the New York World Fair the following year. In *Five Variants of 'Dives and Lazarus'* Vaughan Williams produced an orchestral version of a folk song he had discovered in 1893 together with those 'variants' that he had collected from all parts of the country over the years. A more strictly abstract piece was the *Double Trio*, a divided sextet for strings also composed that year. Although it was well received at its first performance and contained some toughly argued music, together with a whimsical reference to the conductor of the BBC Dance Orchestra – one of the popular radio dance bands of the time – marked 'Homage to Henry Hall', Vaughan Williams was always less certain of his forays into chamber music and eventually withdrew the work for further revision saying the balance 'sounded dull and muddy'. As so often with his revisions, the work would go through many drafts before re-emerging as a *Partita for Double String Orchestra* ten years later.

Throughout the year, there had been diplomatic moves between Britain, France and Hitler concerning the Sudetenland issue, and now the British Prime Minister, Neville Chamberlain, returned from Munich with his famous 'piece of paper' in which he had acceded to Hitler's demands with the promise that the dictator would be sufficiently appeased to maintain 'Peace in our Time'. Many hoped that this would be so, but without much conviction. Already Vaughan Williams was serving on another committee, this time in Dorking, which was attempting to settle refugees from the Nazis in this part of the country. It was no sinecure, for he spent hours doing mundane office work and welcoming the fugitives in person, eventually opening White Gates to some of them. He was now so busy that he had little time to compose, although he was able to attend performances of his works in early 1939, including the *Sea Symphony* in Newcastle and a double bill of *Hugh the Drover* and *Job* in London. He also travelled to Trinity College, Dublin to receive another honorary D.Mus.

The situation in Europe became progressively worse. The Spanish Civil War, which had been such a left-wing *cause célèbre*, ended with defeat for the Republicans and victory for General Franco's Fascists. Emboldened by the success of his protégé, Hitler then invaded the remainder of Czechoslovakia and made demands on Polish territory. The infamous non-aggression pact between the Russian dictator Stalin and Hitler in August removed German obstacles to expansion. Britain and France began to mobilise their Army reserves, air-raid shelters were dug and preparations were made for the defence of London. The country was on a knife-edge but still Chamberlain thought he could call Hitler's bluff, even after Hitler invaded Poland. On 1 September he issued a withdrawal ultimatum which was ignored. On 3 September, appropriately dressed in black and with a high wing collar virtually choking his words, he announced on the radio that Britain was 'consequently at war with Germany'.

Auden wrote in his poem *1st September 1939*:

> ... the clever hopes expire
> Of a low dishonest decade.

11 The Composer in Wartime

The first few months of what later became known as the 'phoney war' were full of petty restrictions as officialdom went through the motions of an emergency. Gas masks were issued, barbed wire barricades and minefields laid along beaches, defence trenches dug along lines of hills, children evacuated from the large cities, black-out orders imposed, whilst people were kept in a permanent state of agitation by air-raid siren drill. Vaughan Williams was sixty-seven, much too old for active service, but he immediately threw himself into every aspect of war work where he felt he might help. There were his committees for refugees and for the release of interned alien musicians, his tireless letter-writing, and, although the Dorking Halls had now been transformed into an emergency government store, he also began organising recitals in a hotel in Dorking for displaced people and eventually popular concerts for the servicemen stationed nearby. He handed over the field at the back of his house for allotments, cultivated a patch himself and set up hen-houses, then found a handcart which he pushed tirelessly round the streets of Dorking collecting anything that might be recycled for the war effort. Still he was not satisfied, worrying that his role as a musician should be more in tune with the people's needs. Restrictions had been introduced limiting the amount of music played on the radio, but he was able to contribute talks, one of which, 'The Composer in Wartime' broadcast in 1940, laid out his own thoughts and suggestions:

What is the composer to do in wartime? ... Some lucky devils are, I believe, able to go on with their art as if nothing had happened. To them the war is merely an irritating intrusion on their spiritual and therefore their true life. I have known young composers refer with annoyance to this 'boring war'. Such a phrase as this, I confess, shocks me, but it set me wondering what their point of view was and whether it was a possible one.

Whatever this war is, it is not boring. It may have been unnecessary, it may be wrong, but it cannot be ignored: it will affect our lives and those of generations to come. Is it then not worth while even for the most aloof artist to take some stock of the situation, to ensure at least that if and when the war ends he will be able to continue composing ...? What will be the musical material on which the composer of the future can count? It will be no use writing elaborate orchestral pieces if there are no orchestras left to play them, or subtle string quartets if there are no subtle instrumentalists available.

One thing, I think, we can be sure of, no bombs or blockades can rob us of our vocal chords; there will always remain for us the oldest and greatest of musical instruments, the human voice.

After considering whether composers can at all be 'useful' in a wartime context, as poets could be for propaganda or painters for camouflage, and wondering whether music should retain its spiritual dimension to 'reserve for us a place where sanity can again find a home when she returns to her own', he suggests that the craft of music could produce material for 'the modest amateur' as the madrigalists of an earlier age had done, but to be used in darkened homes or in dug-outs. He also cites the example of the German 'Home Music' movement, for which many famous composers had written and arranged music for amateurs to use at home.

With the symphony on which he was still slowly working, Vaughan Williams was already producing the spiritual music 'where sanity can find a home' and he soon found a way to contribute music for general use. He wrote *Household Music* based on hymn tunes for four unspecified instruments and began searching for texts for songs which might be performed with or without instruments.

Another opportunity was offered early in 1940 when the music director of London Films, Muir Mathieson, asked him to write the score for the feature film *49th Parallel*. Vaughan Williams was an inveterate cinema-goer, interested in everything from high-budget extravaganzas down to the humblest Mickey Mouse cartoon, and he was aware of the possibilities of the medium when handled by such masters as the Russian director Eisenstein or by Arthur Bliss. He was also aware of the problems Holst had encountered when writing film music but he was fascinated by this new method of 'giving music back to the people' calling it 'a splendid discipline', and rose to the challenge perfectly, bringing his full symphonic guns to bear on music which required flexibility and contrast often within a few bars but could be cut or otherwise mutilated at the whim of a director. He invented the term 'plug tune' by which he meant any theme repeated in a score and in his essay on the subject he wrote:

Ernest Irving and Ralph Vaughan Williams, a photograph taken by Muir Mathieson.

When the film composer comes down to brass tracks he finds himself confronted with a rigid time-sheet. The producer says, 'I want forty seconds of music here.' This means forty, not thirty-nine or forty-one. The picture rolls on relentlessly like Fate. If the music is too short it will stop dead just before the culminating kiss; if it is too long, it will still be registering intense emotion while the screen is already showing the comic man putting on his mother-in-law's breeches.

He also found that:

... you must not be horrified if you find that a passage which you intended to portray the villain's mad revenge has been used by the musical director to illustrate the cats being driven out of the dairy. The truth is that within certain limits any music can be made to fit any situation.

97

49th Parallel was to be the first of a series of film scores he wrote for full-length films and he would also supply music for shorter Ministry of Information films. High-quality music was much more in demand in wartime than usual, 'classical' music being greatly appreciated amongst an emotionally charged population and although the cinema was an area of popular entertainment, it soon started flirting with a hybrid hero – the classical composer who was also in the armed forces. This matinee idol was almost invariably writing a concerto in the style of Rachmaninov which gave the film composer an opportunity to indulge in tense emotional pieces such as the *Warsaw Concerto* and *The Dream of Olwen*. By writing music for less overtly romantic films, Vaughan Williams was nonetheless providing quality music to an audience avid for more than the musical jingoism of the earlier war.

He managed to borrow the Dorking Halls for a much-reduced Leith Hill Festival in 1940, performing oratorios by Handel, and organised a performance of his *Mass in G Minor* in St Paul's Cathedral for a distressed musicians' charity, but by now the war had begun in earnest, with frequent air raids on London, and the possibility of being bombed along any portion of the south-east flight path. Earlier in the year, Honorine had married and moved to London, and the Vaughan Williams's worst fears were realised when they heard that she had been one of the earliest victims of the raids.

Bad news continued throughout the summer with the defeat of the Allies in France, but the remarkable rescue of the bulk of British forces from the beaches of Dunkirk by flotillas of civilian boats seemed to snatch some measure of comfort from the jaws of defeat. In the autumn, the Battle of Britain occurred during which Royal Air Force Spitfires and Hurricanes managed to repulse a German invasion force, but despite these events being hailed as a propaganda coup for the British, the country knew that it had been dangerously close to defeat. Perhaps only Hitler's ill-judged decision to attack Russia saved it from further major assault, but Britain knew nothing of such plans until the following summer after Hitler had invaded Greece and the Balkan states.

Throughout this dark period of anxiety and isolation, the new Prime Minister, Winston Churchill, supplied encouraging rhetoric and musicians continued to offer relief from the everyday terrors of war. As the bombing of London and other major cities increased and Hitler's Axis allies advanced to cut a swathe through Europe and North Africa, the Promenade Concerts continued, scheduled to finish before the night air-raids began, and Vaughan Williams helped the pianist Myra Hess organise those lunchtime recitals in London's National Gallery that became a legendary focus of peace. He also managed to cram the Leith Hill Festival into Dorking's parish church of St Martin's, where reduced versions of *The Messiah* and Bach's *St Matthew Passion* became much-loved favourites.

Russia allied with Britain after Hitler's lightning invasion and by the end of 1941, America had entered the war, with Britain beginning to be used as the base for European operations. This seemed to augur hope, although the air raids continued to sap morale. Vaughan Williams's music for *49th Parallel* was such a success that in 1942 he was asked to write the score for the more overtly wartime film, *Coastal Command* about the aircraft guarding the island during 1940-41. He remarked that, basically, he had 'ignored the details and sought only to intensify the spirit of the situation by a continuous stream of music' writing at least one hair-raising sequence depicting the sinking of an enemy ship in a generally exciting score. There was another war film, *The Story of a Flemish Farm* and, in continuing pastoral vein, The National Trust commissioned him to write for *The People's Land*, a film extolling the beauties of the English countryside. In each, he was aware that the patriotic and rural element was heightened for propaganda purposes, but films such as these helped to maintain the morale of a nation at a time when a more questioning view would have been inappropriate, and they also served as a focus for his more deeply-rooted nationalism, which he saw as part of a wider understanding between the nations. He wrote that year:

I believe that the love of one's country, one's language, one's customs, one's religion, are essential to our national health. We may laugh at these things, but we love them none the less. Indeed, it is one of our national characteristics and one which I should be sorry to see disappear, that we laugh at what we love. This is something that a foreigner can never fathom, but it is out of such characteristics, these hard knots in our timber, that we can help to build up a united Europe and a world federation.

His film music often shared the same emotional or thematic climate as other compositions he was writing at the time, and parts of it were sometimes adapted to other uses. In the scherzo of his *String Quartet No. 2 in A minor* which he began writing at the request of his friend Jean Stewart, chief viola player of the Menges Quartet, he drew on part of the score for *49th Parallel*. He only managed to complete the first two movements that winter and sent them to Jean on her twenty-ninth birthday in February 1943, writing 'the scherzo refuses to materialise,' although this was only a temporary block and he was able to complete the part later in the year. Other music written at this time included a motet, *Valiant for Truth* and songs to words by Shelley. The symphony was also nearing completion. Although he no longer had Holst to advise him as he had with his *Fourth Symphony*, he had collected a few sympathetic friends to listen to piano reductions of his scores, and had the help of a series of copyists who unravelled his often chaotically written manuscripts. Nevertheless, he missed his old friend's advice, and was doubly cautious before releasing anything so important as the *Symphony No.5 in D*.

News from North Africa, where the Germans were being driven

Ralph stand next to Gerald Finzi outside St Martin's church, Dorking.

back, seemed to promise a turning point in the Allies' fortunes, but amidst the greyness of London Vaughan Williams did not expect the celebrations that attended his seventieth birthday celebrations in October. Despite wartime privations the BBC broadcast his music for a week, the Menges Quartet devoted a National Gallery concert to him and there was a concert at the Royal Albert Hall which included *Dona Nobis Pacem* and the *Sea Symphony*. Tributes and letters of congratulation lauded him for his music and for his qualities as a good, unpretentious man, but one who would stand like a rock by his principles. Yet he enjoyed the private celebrations most of all: intimate luncheon parties with friends and the gift of a song cycle from his younger friend, the composer Gerald Finzi. Although he had reached an age at which many men would have considered their best years over, he was in good general health with his energy and invention undimmed. His cousin Ralph Wedgwood had written to him: 'The last Rembrandts were the best, the last Titians the most surprising.' He certainly had a few more surprises up his sleeve.

When Vaughan Williams conducted the *Symphony No. 5 in D* at a broadcast Promenade Concert in June 1943, it surprised many who had expected something as tense and explosive as the Fourth. It is unusual nevertheless, with movements entitled Preludio, Scherzo, Romanza and Passacaglia and the serenity of Bunyan's inner vision produced a meditation on pure peace as gratifying to its listeners as any reflection of warlike sounds would have been disturbing. Adrian Boult wrote to Vaughan Williams after the première:

… its serene loveliness is completely satisfying in these times and shows, as only music can, what we must work for when this madness is over. I look forward to another performance and to the privilege of doing it myself some time soon.

Shostakovich's *Leningrad Symphony* had swept the world as a cry of defiance from the besieged city and had stood as a symbol of Russian hope in the face of the German assault on their country. In its own utterly different way, Vaughan Williams's *Fifth Symphony* now symbolised the inner strength of the English at its very core although its music seemed as much a pointer to the future, when 'a healing of the nations' might once again be possible, as a longing for the certainties of the past.

As summer progressed, the Allies entered Italy and began pushing north whilst the German armies were being driven out of Russia, but it seemed as though it would be a long time before the madness would be over as the relentless bombing of Britain continued unabated. Throughout the war, White Gates was a refuge from London for many guests. In addition to R.O. Morris there was for a short time the evacuee daughter of Vaughan Williams's old comrade and friend Harry Steggles, there were assorted nephews, honorary nieces and friends who came and went, and one particular friend and helper Ursula Wood, who was given sympathetic shelter following the death of her husband. Despite the danger, Vaughan Williams still visited London occasionally, busying himself with committee work, including one for the performance of new composers' works, attending concerts, visiting friends and lunching with them in small musicians' restaurants or taking in a film or play. Returning to the peace of his untidy study in Dorking, Vaughan Williams looked to the same healing world as his *Fifth Symphony* and began writing a *Concerto for Oboe and Strings* which reflected the same warmth and longing but with a more bucolic relaxation. Two of the three movements hint at this in their titles – *Rondo Pastorale* and *Minuet and Musette* – whilst the finale contains music originally rejected for the scherzo of the *Fifth Symphony*. In addition to working on this, he supplied music for a radio adaptation of *The Pilgrim's Progress* using music that he was also expanding into the full-length opera on which he had worked intermittently since the early years of the century. He also rehearsed the *St Matthew Passion* for the following spring's Leith Hill Festival, where it had become a regular feature.

By 1944, the war had reached a desperate climax with the terrifying V1 flying bombs being launched in droves across Britain and the Allies preparing for the D-Day landings in France. In the summer, Vaughan Williams's brother Hervey died leaving Leith Hill Place to him. Many would have envied him the position, but he dreaded the responsibility, for not only was there the great house with all its ancestral effects, but estates and tenants to look after and Vaughan Williams knew he was not cut out to be a country squire. He wrestled with the idea, but decided in the end to hand his inheritance to the National Trust, keeping the artefacts intact in the house apart from a few private mementos. When he discovered that the first tenants of the house were to be his cousin Ralph Wedgwood and his wife, he knew that he had done the right thing.

Sir Henry Wood receives a volume full of tributes for his seventy-fifth birthday.

The *Oboe Concerto* was first performed by its dedicatee, Leon Goossens, in September, furthering the sense of peace that the *Fifth Symphony* had begun and few weeks later, on his seventy-second birthday, the Menges Quartet premièred Vaughan Williams's *String Quartet No.2* twice at a National Gallery concert. Vaughan Williams had finished the work with an Epilogue marked 'Greetings from Joan to Jean'. Jean was obviously Jean Stewart, but the enigmatic Joan was none other than Joan of Arc, the main theme being taken from music for a projected film about the French martyr which was never made. Although this last movement is resigned and peaceful with something of the atmosphere of the *Fifth Symphony*, much of the rest of the music reflects the harsh uncertainties of this bleak period and has a troubled, restless feel. The viola is given a prominent part throughout, but the music is much more than an occasional gift and stands as a significant addition to the string quartet repertoire in its own right.

As the Allies pushed on through northern Europe into Germany itself, it was obvious that the war would soon end, despite the added horror of V2 flying bombs wreaking devastation before they could even be heard. The BBC commissioned Vaughan Williams to write a *Thanksgiving for Victory* for which he collated different texts that considered the morality of war as much as relief for its ending and in such a way avoided mere triumphalism. Whilst he was writing it, he saw Laurence Olivier's film of *Henry V* with its prestigious colour, use of experimental stylisation in various sequences and extraordinarily effective music by William Walton. The play, perhaps Shakespeare's most patriotic, dealt with topics and themes similar to those that Vaughan Williams was considering and he included a section from it in his commission. The score was laid out for the experimental forces of narrator, chorus and orchestra, and was first performed on the radio on the first Sunday after the unconditional surrender of Germany on 9 May 1945. Churchill announced to the people that they might enjoy 'a brief period of rejoicing' before the reconstruction of a devastated land should begin. Meanwhile, the war continued in the East against Japan.

Looking back on the period, there seemed little to rejoice about: Vaughan Williams had lost old friends, millions had died, whilst London and many other British cities had been blitzed almost beyond recognition with magnificent buildings destroyed, including the Queen's Hall, scene of so many early triumphs. As news came in from Europe, it was clear that all the great cities Vaughan Williams had loved – Berlin, Dresden, Hamburg and Lübeck among them – had been razed to the ground, and unimaginable scenes of horror filled the newsreels with the opening of the Nazi death camps.

Yet more horror of unimaginable magnitude occurred on the 6 and 9 of August: the first atom bombs were dropped on the Japanese cities of Hiroshima and Nagasaki, effectively ending the war but initiating a new Age of Anxiety. A sense of paranoia would

102

soon grow amongst former allies as they divided the spoils of war. It would not be long before Winston Churchill would make his famous reference to an 'iron curtain' descending on Europe and, with opposing arsenals bristling with nuclear weapons, the possibility of global annihilation began to seem a very real threat. It was in this mood that Vaughan Williams began writing a new symphony which would return to the sound world of the Fourth but, as he said, with his latest musical experiments 'recollected in tranquillity'.

12 A Solitary Peak

The post-war Labour government began the task of reconstruction with a package of social reforms and functional rebuilding, but years of grim austerity were to follow, with rationing still imposed. The few pleasures that people could afford revolved largely around cinemas and dance halls, and Vaughan Williams continued to provide music for the former with a new score for *Stricken Peninsula*. Like much of the music he produced for films, he echoed the ideas he was using in his more abstract music, and the new symphony seemed to grow out of this testing ground as much as from his own emotions.

Music, which had been such a comfort during the war years, also continued to increase in popularity and the 1945 season of Albert Hall Promenade Concerts included the first complete cycle of Vaughan Williams's five symphonies. There were younger men including Benjamin Britten and Michael Tippett who were coming to the fore and were producing vibrant and interesting new music, not least in the field of opera, where *Peter Grimes* and *The Midsummer Marriage* continued in the tradition Vaughan Williams and Holst had begun. There were also other fine English symphonists to be heard, including Arnold Bax who had produced a steady stream of works in this form, William Walton whose symphony was still considered a powerful exercise in the medium, Edmund Rubbra, Havergal Brian and George Lloyd. The variety and appeal of Vaughan Williams's symphonies put them in a class of their own, however, and with his fame consolidated through his war work, and his tireless contribution to the furtherance of British music old and new, it was now realised that he was the leading British composer of the age.

Yet having reached this pinnacle, he was determined not to become remote. He still refused the knighthood that most successful musicians regarded as their right, sensing that if he was to be an Establishment figure he must not be buried by its empty pomp. He remained approachable, attracted to people by their qualities rather than their positions. To his neighbours in Dorking, he seemed no different from hundreds of other elderly men, with his shock of white hair and portly build, pottering about in his garden or strolling into town dressed casually in old clothes, and to many young people to whom he had shown encouragement and kindness, he was simply 'Uncle Ralph'. His work in the community had brought music to everyone, and he relished the story of the messenger boy who delivered a parcel, 'hesitated a moment then

Conducting the *London Symphony* in the Albert Hall, 1946.

added, "When's the Passion?"' Although he was beginning to be slower and more deliberate in his movements and was also experiencing the onset of that most terrible of all complaints for a musician – hearing difficulties – his stamina would have put many a younger man to shame. Rising early every day to compose, helping the nurses with his virtually crippled wife, travelling to London to rehearse orchestras or discuss his latest film score, his seemingly uneventful life probably had the inner fulfilment of a man at the height of his creative powers.

In 1946 he produced the film score for *The Loves of Joanna Godden* the story of a woman farmer on Romney Marshes which contains music of chilling intensity. The *Symphony No.6 in E minor* was almost complete and was played through in its piano reduction to a select group of friends that summer. Other important events included the first professional production of *Sir John in Love* given by Sadler's Wells and the première of a new work, *Introduction and Fugue* for two pianos performed by its dedicatees, Cyril Smith and Phyllis Sellick. They also gave the first performance of the revised *Piano Concerto*, now rearranged for two pianos and orchestra. Its monumental percussive outer movements seemed to lie better between the two instruments and its tough and sinewy texture reminded audiences of the earlier Vaughan Williams while also pointing towards the symphony that he was orchestrating at the time.

In addition to these compositions, he spent part of 1947 writing occasional music and providing alternative versions of earlier works. He wrote an anthem for the commemoration of a Battle of Britain chapel in Westminster Abbey, *The Souls of the Righteous*, and arranged part of the *Job* ballet music to words from the Book of Job for choral performance. The piano repertoire received an arrangement of part of his music for the film *49th Parallel* and he was also writing a new finale for his rearrangement of the *Double Trio* as a *Partita for Double String Orchestra*. That year also saw the return of the Leith Hill Festival to the Dorking Halls, with contingents from twenty-four surrounding districts. Bach's *Mass in B minor* in Vaughan Williams's own metrical English translation was the work sung by the competing choirs, and he was also able to introduce the *St John Passion* at a separate concert. Performances of *The Poisoned Kiss* and *The Shepherds of the Delectable Mountains* were given at the Royal College of Music and Sadler's Wells respectively and he conducted his *Fifth Symphony* and *Magnificat* at the Gloucester Three Choirs Festival, returning in time for the

Leith Hill Musical Festival in the Dorking Halls in 1947.

106

celebrations attending his seventy-fifth birthday in October. There was a party at the Dorking Halls where the *Sea Symphony* was also performed, the *London Symphony, Sancta Civitas* and *Flos Campi* were broadcast on the radio and there were official greetings and letters from friends and admirers from all over the world. The year also held one special event: Ralph and Adeline's Golden Wedding Anniversary, which they celebrated privately. The pair were as devoted as ever, with Adeline as sharply critical of Ralph's music as Holst had been although she was now so incapacitated that she was confined to a wheelchair and could only make infrequent, painful excursions to the outside world by car.

That year Vaughan Williams accepted a commission to write the score for what appeared the most ambitious film project he had attempted: the story of the tragic expedition to the Antarctic undertaken by Captain Scott's party in 1912. Vaughan Williams had been forty when he had originally heard news of the disaster and he was now moved afresh by such courage in the face of natural adversity and by the futility of wasted lives. Although he had never visited the region, pictorial references and a sympathetic imagination soon brought music from his pen in his most noble vein whilst giving him the opportunity to use unusual combinations of instruments to describe an ice-bound, windswept landscape.

The *Partita for Double String Orchestra* was broadcast in March 1948 with Adrian Boult conducting. A month later he directed the BBC Symphony Orchestra in the first performance of the *Symphony No.6 in E minor*. Its first three movements exploding with savage energy, followed without a break by one of the quietest and bleakest of epilogues seeming to depict a devastated landscape more remote even than that of Holst's *Egdon Heath*, gave rise to much speculation about its 'meaning', although everyone agreed that this was a towering masterpiece. Once more it confounded those who thought they knew the stage Vaughan Williams had arrived at in his output and many thought that the benedictory mood of the *Fifth Symphony* had been shattered by the revelations of the Second World War's atrocities and the advancing nuclear arms race, one critic later calling it Vaughan Williams's 'War Symphony'. Vaughan Williams had not helped to shed light on the matter, writing one of his typically flippant programme notes, referring at one point to a jazzy xylophone and saxophone interlude being inverted 'to the delight of everyone including the composer' but he later wrote:

I do not believe in meanings and mottoes, as you know, but I think we can get in words nearest to the substance of my last movement in 'We are such stuff as dreams are made on, and our little life is rounded with a sleep'.

This reference to Shakespeare's *The Tempest* does not illuminate the music much more than Beethoven's gruff 'Thus Fate knocks on the door' when asked about the 'meaning' of his own *Fifth Symphony*, but perhaps the emotional range and complexity of the score are indescribable in words. Whatever the message it conveyed, the work went immediately into the repertoire, receiving more than a hundred performances over the next two years and, like Elgar's *First Symphony* 'going round the world', giving recognition to the fact that this was the most international of his symphonies.

He had come a long way since the days when his student scores had been corrected by his old tutor, Parry, for whose centenary in May he wrote a suitably choral tribute *A Prayer to the Father of Heaven* to Skelton's words. He was also at the Sheldonian Theatre in Oxford for the celebrations and later wrote:

What about Parry as a composer? Potentially, I believe, he was among the greatest. There is however one outstanding exception. I fully believe – and keeping the achievements of Byrd, Purcell and Elgar firmly before my eyes – *Blest Pair of Sirens* is the finest musical work that has come out of these islands.

Later in the year Vaughan Williams was at Covent Garden for the first post-war production of *Job* with Robert Helpmann as Satan. Although John Piper's sets did not live up to the original Blakean production, the house was full and Vaughan Williams was moderately satisfied with the effect. Later that year he conducted a concert performance of *Job* in Worcester Cathedral during the Three Choirs Festival. On this occasion, he was accompanied by his friend Ursula Wood and they spent a few days afterwards revisiting his childhood home in Down Ampney, then visiting those parts of Shropshire made famous by Housman's poetry before returning to Dorking.

After delivering the score for *Scott of the Antarctic* in the autumn, Vaughan Williams returned to the opera he had been writing for nearly forty years – *The Pilgrim's Progress* – incorporating most of *The Shepherds of the Delectable Mountains* in the final act. The music was now near completion, although to release such a long labour of love to the world would require delicate timing and Vaughan Williams, not yet certain of the response it would receive, continued to rewrite and revise the score. Whilst in Dorking, Ralph and Adeline heard of the death of R.O. Morris from a heart attack, which severed another long link with the past.

Always alert to new possibilities, Vaughan Williams now seemed to set himself a series of musical challenges. Whilst considering old projects for operas, he had unearthed his sketches for an opera based on Matthew Arnold's poem *The Scholar Gypsy* concerning an Oxford undergraduate who had left his studies and taken to the roads. He had long abandoned any notion of making anything dramatic out of this basically static and meditative poem, but he now decided to create a work for speaker, orchestra and wordless choir based on extracts from the poem and the poet's equally

Ursula Wood.

108

lyrical *Thyrsis*. This was an unusual experiment, but he relished the task as with all the challenges he set himself. Another unusual challenge he rose to in 1949 was to write a work similar to Beethoven's *Choral Fantasia* for piano, chorus and orchestra, but the *Fantasia (quazi variazione) on the 'Old 104th' Psalm Tune* grew beyond the bounds of even that master's experiments to explore every possibility of the theme and every area of his musical forces. A further challenge was a commission for a piece to be played in schools for the whole range of musicians from advanced to virtual beginners. He responded by using the eighteenth century form of the *Concerto Grosso* with the music laid out in such a way that each part of the string orchestra had something interesting to play in a tuneful and satisfying manner. In each of these works it is clear that Vaughan Williams was relishing all the techniques at his disposal and stretching himself into even more distant regions. But he was still willing to provide 'occasional' music when the demand was there, including the music he wrote for a pageant to commemorate the four hundredth anniversary of his *alma mater*, Charterhouse, in the summer of 1949.

Scott of the Antarctic opened, with Vaughan Williams's passionately descriptive music intensified by the harsh beauty of colour photography. As Vaughan Williams watched it, he realised his score was on a more symphonic, spiritual and heroic level than earlier music he had written for film, and its worth was recognised when it was singled out for various awards, including first prize at the Prague Film Festival. He was not willing to confine it to a suite as he had done with his music for the *Flemish Farm*, not only because that had received an indifferent reception, but because the nobility and tragedy of the theme together with the emotional commitment he had given to it demanded nothing less than a symphony. If a great film would never be built up on the basis of music as he had hoped it might, perhaps great music could emerge from a film. Shortly afterwards he began considering how he might reshape *Scott of the Antarctic* into a *Sinfonia Antartica* which would be a new departure for him – a hybrid of symphony and symphonic poem.

He still enjoyed the discipline of writing music to precise order and was thus pleased to accept a commission from the BBC Radio Drama Department to provide incidental music for the 'Sunday Serial'. He and Adeline both enjoyed listening to these abridged versions and would then read the novels out loud to one another and to friends. Although *The Mayor of Casterbridge* was not one of Vaughan Williams's favourites amongst Hardy's works, he provided music for it in a week saying in his typically disarming way: 'Do what you like with it. Play it backwards if you want to.' Once more, he proved to be the supreme craftsman for, as the producer remarked, 'he had summed up the whole of Hardy's masterpiece and foreseen every need.'

One of the accolades bestowed on public figures at the time, was to be sculpted by a semi-official if controversial sculptor,

Jacob Epstein, and Vaughan Williams was now singled out for this honour. His strong but benign features lent themselves exactly to the artist's medium which produced a dignified portrait of the composer at the height of his fame and powers, and Epstein has left a reminiscence which sums up his sitter's personality:

Here was the master with whom no one would venture to dispute. He reminded one in appearance of some eighteenth-century admiral whose word was law. Notwithstanding I found him the epitome of courtesy and consideration, and I was impressed by the logic and acuteness of everything he discoursed upon and was made aware of his devotion to an art as demanding as sculpture.

Vaughan Williams enjoyed his sittings with Epstein, but when the famous photographer Karsh of Ottawa arrived to photograph him that same year he found the whole exercise much more trying. It was worth the effort, however, for the photograph captured the craggy face in all its humanity, a twinkle of humour in the eyes lightening the monumental pose.

By 1950, the reconstruction of the country was proceeding with some measure of success, although the drab utilitarianism of 'temporary' prefabricated bungalows and the open scars of bomb sites would continue to disfigure cities for many years to come. There was a feeling that the nation needed a focus for future development and, since the centenary of the Great Exhibition would occur in 1951, efforts had been made since 1949 to recreate a modern counterpart to Prince Albert's ambitious showcase of British ingenuity planned, as the King would say in his opening speech 'as a visible sign of national achievement and confidence'. The Festival of Britain was intended to cover a large area near Waterloo Station in London where contemporary styles would be used to construct a Dome of Discovery flanked by pavilions containing the best of Industry plus Scientific and Technical wonders for an admiring populace, the whole presided over by a strange upwardly soaring 'Skylon'. The Arts would also be represented by theatre and music, but it was not to be all high-minded, for frivolity would be provided by an enormous Pleasure Garden in Battersea Park.

The project that interested Vaughan Williams was the construction of a new concert hall. Although the Festival Hall would eventually become one of the finest concert halls in London (despite originally possessing a dry acoustic), he soon began to have doubts about its architectural idiom, which the architect brusquely explained 'expresses today, not a past age', and since he also disagreed with other more musical parts of the project, he decided not to give it his support. However he did accept a Festival of Britain commission to write a work for the National Festival of Schools' Music to be held in the Albert Hall. This became the cantata *The Sons of Light*, to words by Ursula Wood.

The *St Matthew Passion* was sung at the Leith Hill Festival as usual, but with added relevance, this being Bach's bicentenary. Vaughan Williams was also involved in two other amateur events that year, both staged in the Albert Hall: the first a folk song festival performed by Women's Institute choirs for which he had arranged folk songs in a seasonal layout, and the second a concert given by young musicians from rural schools during which they played his specially composed *Concerto Grosso* with evident enjoyment. The Three Choirs Festival in Gloucester also provided a platform for a new work. Following a performance of the *Sixth Symphony*, Vaughan Williams conducted his new *Fantasia on the 'Old 104th'* with his amanuensis and copyist Michael Mullinar playing the taxing piano part.

At last it seemed that Covent Garden was interested in staging *The Pilgrim's Progress* and Vaughan Williams began negotiations which lasted most of the rest of the year, for problems seem to have occurred about how to bring an essentially static, dreamlike opera to life on the stage. 'The opera is to be acted almost like a ritual and not in the ordinary dramatic sense,' Vaughan Williams wrote. In fact, it was not billed as an opera at all but 'A Morality in a Prologue, Four Acts and an Epilogue', although he realised that much that he regarded as symbolic, including monsters such as Apollyon which he would have preferred to be a series of lights and shadows, had to be visually represented for dramatic effect. At last, at the end of April 1951, beginning a run that would extend into the Festival of Britain, the night Vaughan Williams had waited for since his youth occurred and *The Pilgrim's Progress* opened at Covent Garden.

The performance went well and no-one doubted the beauty and aptness of the music but, after the curtain calls, Vaughan Williams sensed that the reception was only polite. The newspapers confirmed his fears the following day with distant praise and outright hostility. Perhaps this 'morality' was out of tune with the whole Festival of Britain ethos, and perhaps some saw what Benjamin Britten had called Vaughan Williams's 'pi and artificial mysticism' in it. The physical world of post-war Britain was one of pock-marked ugliness, but Britten and other critics did not understand that Vaughan Williams's vision, like Bunyan's and Blake's, lay 'beyond the unknown region' in a parallel universe, distant from but contiguous with the cars and urban sprawl that were disfiguring the landscape, and further still from the materialistic thrust of 1950s England.

Vaughan Williams, although hurt by this indifference to his most deeply cherished project, philosophically remarked, 'They don't like it, they won't like it and perhaps they never will like it, but it's the sort of opera I wanted to write, and there it is.' There were further performances, a radio broadcast which possibly suited the music better, and later the cast took it on tour with new amendments and additions by Vaughan Williams himself, but it did not achieve real popularity.

Hugh the Drover and *Sir John in Love* were both performed at this time, however, and there was a great deal of music-making attached to the Festival. The opening concert at the Royal Festival Hall included Vaughan Williams's *Serenade to Music* together with Handel, and the inevitable *Pomp and Circumstance* and *Rule Britannia*. For the first time in England a corporation, the London County Council, had commissioned works from such talents as Alan Rawsthorne, William Alwyn and Edmund Rubbra and there was also a competition for young composers, but Vaughan Williams was characteristically more interested in the school children's festival in the Albert Hall where his new cantata *The Sons of Light* was first performed.

On the afternoon of 10 May he attended a performance of *Toward the Unknown Region* at London University. This must have brought back memories of his early composition contests with Holst, who had now been dead for seventeen years but whom he had never ceased to miss. Whilst he listened to the music, the only other person who had been as close to him was also dying. He did not discover until his return to Dorking that evening that Adeline had passed away during the afternoon.

Ralph and Adeline, photograph taken by Ursula in 1950.

112

13 An Indian Summer

At Leith Hill Festival.

Although his wife had been frail for years and had passed through many crises during that time, Vaughan Williams could not have been totally prepared for her loss. In his grief, he turned to close friends, and none was closer than Ursula Wood who had known the couple since 1939 and had been a companion and helper to them both since the death of her husband, as much at home in Dorking as in her London flat. She arrived immediately to help with arrangements and later wrote of Adeline:

When I went to her room next day, taking flowers from the garden, she looked as fragile as the body of a small bird. Her early beauty, her lively mind, her austere discipline, her tenderness and edged wit had dissolved and left no trace on the wrecked face that lay between hyacinths and jonquils on the pillow.

After the funeral, Vaughan Williams threw himself into work. There was the Leith Hill Festival to attend to and the *Sinfonia Antartica* to complete, whilst his household business would be looked after by Ursula when she could spare the time. She also provided him with a room of his own in London so that he could visit the capital more easily. The *Sea Symphony* was performed during the Festival of Britain celebrations and the *Fifth Symphony* at the Three Choirs Festival in Worcester which they attended

On 14th December 1951, Ralph received, from the hands of the Chancellor, Mr Winston Churchill, the first Honorary Doctorate of Music given by the University of Bristol.

Resting on the steps of the Mont St Michel, Brittany.

together, then, after travelling to Bristol University in December to receive an honorary D. Mus from its Chancellor Winston Churchill, Vaughan Williams returned to Dorking to spend the better part of the winter working on the *Sinfonia Antartica*, which he had decided should keep such atmospheric effects as wordless voices and a wind machine. His latest amanuensis, Roy Douglas, worked with him part of the time and soon the music began to take a five-movement shape.

The death of George VI in February 1952 aroused a genuine feeling of loss for a man who had helped sustain the nation through its most difficult years, but the new monarch, Elizabeth II, now became the focus of a feeling of youthful enterprise. People talked of 'a new Elizabethan Age' with all its connotations of world greatness, courage and optimism, and a spectacular coronation was planned for the following year, furthering the work done by the Festival of Britain in fostering a spirit of recovery. Naturally, Vaughan Williams was asked if he would write a *Te Deum* but replied, 'No thank you, I've already written one,' and hoping to bring the congregation into the service suggested that if the Archbishop of Canterbury could be persuaded to include a hymn, he would 'make a mess-up of the Old 100th'. This typically laconic reply was accepted and Vaughan Williams set to work making a splendid version of the hymn including organ, choir, orchestra and extra trumpets. He also agreed to write a more conventional motet, *O Taste and See*, and a part song, *A Garland for the Queen*, for a new collection from various contemporary composers to be modelled on madrigals originally entitled *The Triumphs of Oriana*, written for Elizabeth I.

Ursula Wood had now become his constant support, accompanying him on short breaks and travelling with him to concerts and festivals. In May, she persuaded him to go abroad for the first time since his visit to Germany before the War. There were restrictions on the amount of money British residents could take with them,

John Barbirolli discusses the *Sea Symphony* in the Hallé rehearsal room.

Malcolm Sargent, Ralph
Vaughan Williams and Larry
Adler.

but they decided that a trip to Normandy might be a possibility
on the permitted £25. Although Vaughan Williams had written
extraordinarily effective film music about aeroplanes, he had never
travelled in one before, and he found the new experience
exhilarating. After spending a few days in Paris visiting many of
Vaughan Williams's old familiar haunts, the two travelled by train
and bus to Chartres, St Malo and Mont St Michel before returning
via Rouen to Le Havre and taking the ferry back to England.
Despite the financial privations, it had been a civilised holiday
and one that nostalgically reminded the elderly composer of his
own family holidays in childhood.

They were in Oxford in June for the first performance of *An
Oxford Elegy*, given in Queen's College with Steuart Wilson as the
speaker. The music is nostalgic, and one feels that this is more
appropriate to the mood evoked by Matthew Arnold's poems than
the operatic treatment Vaughan Williams had originally considered.
The composer's friend and biographer Michael Kennedy seems
to agree for he saw in the closing words 'the light we sought is
shining still' a reference to 'the septuagenarian composer remembering
his youth in company with Holst and George Butterworth and
reaffirming the idealism that he never lost'.

In the same year, Vaughan Williams finished the score of the
Sinfonia Antartica and it went into rehearsal with the Hallé
Orchestra under John Barbirolli. With this behind him, Vaughan
Williams turned his hand to a lighter work as relief. Always
interested in the possibilities of new and unusual instruments, he
had accepted a commission from the famous American harmonica
player Larry Adler for a short piece in concerto form. When the
dedicatee played it at the Promenade Concerts in September, the
Romance for Harmonica and Orchestra proved a delightful addition

115

An eightieth birthday portrait at the entrance to The White Gates, portrait by Allan Chappelow MA FRSA.

to the repertoire of an instrument often looked down on as plebeian by more academically minded musicians. Once more, Vaughan Williams was 'giving music back to the people' in recalling with affection and respect the favourite instrument of the men he had known in the army.

October saw his eightieth birthday celebrations stretching over a week. They began with a formal dinner at the Trocadero Restaurant given by the Incorporated Society of Musicians, attended by old friends and colleagues who lauded him with speeches and congratulations. A less formal affair was the concert given in Dorking by participants from many Leith Hill Festivals. *An Oxford Elegy*, *Five Mystical Songs* and the *Benedicite* were all performed and a party followed. The official celebrations occurred in the Festival Hall, where the London County Council had organised a concert before an invited audience. *A Song of Thanksgiving* (as the *Thanksgiving for Victory* was now called), *Flos Campi*, *The Sons of Light* and the *Fifth Symphony* were all conducted by Adrian Boult to tremendous and affectionate applause. Another party followed immediately and hundreds of letters and cards arrived at Dorking.

By January 1953, the *Sinfonia Antartica* was thoroughly rehearsed and the first performance took place on the 14th in the Free Trade Hall, Manchester in the presence of Captain Scott's son, the naturalist Peter Scott, and Ernest Irving, the musical director of Ealing Films who had commissioned the original film score and to whom the new symphony was now dedicated. This was followed shortly by a performance in the Festival Hall, London. Audiences found that the familiar music had been reworked into a satisfying symphonic form which still retained all the tragic nobility and suffering of the film score, yet critics were uncertain. Although Vaughan Williams had re-used some of his film music in the earlier

At these birthday celebrations in Nottingham in 1953, Benjamin Britten and Peter Pears talk to assembled guests.

Queen Elizabeth II passes through Westminster Abbey.

Sixth Symphony he had not done it so overtly as in this work. Here, the film associations were perhaps too close for critical comfort. These were emphasised by the title, by literary texts pointing to important sections, a central movement entitled 'Landscape' and a sequence which included music for penguins. It was clear, however, that once more Vaughan Williams had produced something new in his canon of symphonies and in that respect, as Holst would have said to him, 'At least you haven't repeated yourself.'

After the public ceremonies of his birthday and the applause surrounding the new symphony, one very important ceremony occurred quietly on 7 February when Vaughan Williams married Ursula Wood in a London registry office. They left shortly afterwards for a honeymoon in Italy which, with a ceiling of £25 each would have to be carefully planned once more. After visiting Lake Garda, the couple travelled via Verona and Padua to Venice where they spent the main part of their holiday. The setting was, as Ursula wrote, 'perfect'.

The Coronation, which occurred shortly after their return, was everything that austere post-war Britain required in colour and pageantry. Street parties, carnivals and fireworks enlivened the nation whilst the whole ceremony was filmed for cinema audiences and broadcast live in black-and-white on the newly re-opened television service of the BBC. Sitting in Westminster Abbey, Ralph and Ursula had an excellent view of the proceedings, whose music included Vaughan Williams's innovatory 'Old 100th' sung by the congregation with *obbligato* triumphant trumpets and his more restrained motet *O Taste and See*. Other artistic celebrations included Benjamin Britten's new opera *Gloriana*, set at the court of Elizabeth I, which Ralph and Ursula attended at Covent Garden and a double bill of *Hugh the Drover* and *Riders to the Sea* at Sadler's Wells. Television also provided Vaughan Williams with a new medium when *The Bridal Day*★, the masque he had written in collaboration with Ursula before the War was finally performed on its screens that year. As many of these were no larger than nine inches across, however, Vaughan Williams was not impressed with the effect it made and could not see his allegiance switching from cinema screen and radio to this infant instrument of mass entertainment.

That year, Bach's *St John Passion* had been given again at the Leith Hill Festival and Vaughan Williams decided that he would like to write a similar work, using narrator and chorus but telling the Christmas Story in place of the Passion. He and Ursula worked together on a personal anthology of texts which included carols, poems and biblical narrative to produce the outline of a large work to be entitled *Hodie* (This Day). The work reflected all aspects of the story so that Milton's devotional poem 'The Morning of Christ's Nativity' lies close to the agnostic Thomas Hardy's poem 'The Oxen', which may have been closer to Vaughan Williams's

---

★Re-named Epithalamion in the final (1957) version.

10 Hanover Terrace, Regent's Park. Ralph and Ursula lived here from 1953, and Ralph died here on August 26th 1958.

With Charles Groves at the Winter Gardens, Bournemouth. Photograph by the *Evening Echo*, Bournemouth.

own beliefs. He approached the setting with all the experience of a lifetime's choral composition so that the piece gradually grew into a summing-up of works as diverse as the *Mass in G minor* and *Dona Nobis Pacem*.

Meanwhile Ralph and Ursula decided to leave Dorking for London and took the lease on a magnificent house, No. 10, Hanover Terrace, Nash's crescent overlooking Regent's Park, which suited them perfectly. Not only was it central, but it was roomy enough for all Vaughan Williams's books and papers, there was a garden for the cats and their neighbours were friends of long standing. Throughout his years in Dorking, Vaughan Williams had always resented his exile from London, considering himself a Londoner first and foremost. Although it was true that Surrey and Leith Hill Place were his childhood homes, the landscape beneath the North Downs was no longer that of his youth, sullied even in the 1950s by developments that would eventually damage its fragile beauty, prophetic of the present day's airports and motorways. Vaughan Williams did not need the external landscape to inspire him, for his own visionary landscape, both English and universal, lay, as it does with all who could respond to that aspect of his music, on a distant level of the mind and could be tapped into as much in London as in the diminishing fields of 'pastoral' England. He would continue to be involved in the Leith Hill Festival as a guest conductor and intended to visit his cousin at Leith Hill Place occasionally, but otherwise he considered this chapter in his life mercifully closed, and he could look forward to taking part in London life more fully as he soon found that many old friends, pupils and colleagues were still there to welcome him. Amongst the new social gatherings he inaugurated were what he now called 'singeries' involving the singing of madrigals in his home on selected occasions, and there were dozens of concerts and theatrical performances to attend.

After finishing *Hodie*, Vaughan Williams began work on another

Philip Catellet tries out the Tuba Concerto.

Conducting in Worcester Cathedral, 1954.

symphony and a *Tuba Concerto*. These new compositions were extensions of his interest in neglected instruments following on the experiments in the *Sinfonia Antartica* and the harmonica *Romance*. The *Tuba Concerto* was written for Philip Catelinet and fully exploits the instrument's potential with tuneful music, whilst the *Eighth Symphony* became a joyous celebration of the power of percussion. He was also working on a more conventional chamber work, a *Violin Sonata in A minor* for the violinist Frederick Grinke, who had done much to champion *The Lark Ascending* through the years.

Long-playing 'unbreakable' records and 'high fidelity' sound were now replacing the short, scratchy 78 recordings of earlier years and a new project was launched by the Decca company to record the seven symphonies Vaughan Williams had completed. This was a massive project requiring much of his time, as he attended the sessions conducted by Adrian Boult and the London Philharmonic Orchestra, but it was one that he found absorbing as he realised the potential of the new medium for disseminating lengthy works in light-weight convenient format. These projects plus a forthcoming production of *The Pilgrim's Progress* in Cambridge kept him busy throughout the winter. Most of the cast were undergraduates, with the title role being sung by John Noble who was reading Physics, and, when the work was finally produced throughout a week in February, it was such a success that Noble took up singing as his full-time occupation. Vaughan Williams was delighted that his life-long work on the score had finally received a worthy production.

A further holiday in Italy was now planned, and Ralph and Ursula left in May for Pisa, Florence, Siena and Rome, travelling by train through the Italian landscape and sight-seeing relentlessly, especially in Rome, which Vaughan Williams had never visited before. Hardly had they returned from the Eternal City at the end of May than he began preparing for a return visit to America in the autumn, where he had been invited to give a coast-to-coast lecture trip arranged by Keith Falkner, a professor of music at Cornell University. This and the new symphony, plus rehearsals for the first performance of *Hodie* at the Three Choirs Festival in Worcester took up most of his time. After the new choral work had received its first performance in September with Vaughan Williams conducting, he and Ursula immediately set off by boat for New York.

Once more, Vaughan Williams enjoyed staying in the city before the couple set off through New England to Cornell University where he gave his first lectures on 'The Making of Music', attended with the usual American hospitality and enthusiasm. The next stop was in Toronto, Canada and Vaughan Williams was able to revisit Niagara Falls before heading to the Ann Arbor campus of the University of Michigan where he spent his eighty-second birthday lecturing. The birthday was celebrated by a private dinner party and a concert of his choral works which included the *Serenade to Music*. In London, the occasion was marked by Frederick Grinke and Michael Mullinar who gave the first performance of Vaughan Williams's *Violin Sonata* in a BBC radio broadcast.

It took three days to travel from Ann Arbor by train to Los Angeles, where Vaughan Williams lectured at the University before the couple left for Santa Barbara to rest in a hotel close to the Pacific Ocean. Whilst there, Vaughan Williams was delighted to attend an intriguing performance of *Riders to the Sea* given at the University in both the original play and his own operatic version. Following this, the couple travelled by train to the Grand Canyon, which Vaughan Williams considered the highlight of his tour and which he had been anticipating immensely. He was not disappointed with its awe-inspiring and otherworldly splendour and spent two days exploring it from every accessible angle.

Returning to Cornell University, where they now based themselves, Vaughan Williams busied himself with rehearsals for concerts with both the University and the Buffalo symphony orchestras. They gave performances of the *London Symphony* and the *Sancta Civitas* and Vaughan Williams was able to include the *Tallis Fantasia* and *The Wasps Overture* amongst other works performed. Although his deafness was now becoming more troublesome, making conducting an increasing chore, the huge audiences gave him standing ovations. The tour ended in New York from where Vaughan Williams travelled to Yale University for its music department's centenary celebrations. Here he gave his last lecture and was presented with the same honour as Holst had received beforehand – the prestigious Howland Memorial Prize awarded to 'a citizen of any country in recognition of some marked distinction in the field of literature or the fine arts'. Thus, much wealthier than they had been when they arrived and glowing with all the sights

In Buffalo, being feted by Mitzi and Josef Krips.

120

they had seen and the kindnesses they had received during their journey, Ralph and Ursula returned to England in December.

Still writing 'music for use', Vaughan Williams composed an occasional piece for the Salvation Army Brass Band a *Prelude on Three Welsh Hymn Tunes* and found that, more substantially, he had nearly completed his new symphony. Roy Douglas came to help him order the manuscript and there followed intense consultations on his 'new tune' as Vaughan Williams laconically called it. A short break in Cornwall at Easter was followed later in the year by yet another foreign holiday in the autumn, this time to Greece.

The discomforts of his earlier travels in the country as a military man were not duplicated as Ralph and Ursula approached Athens

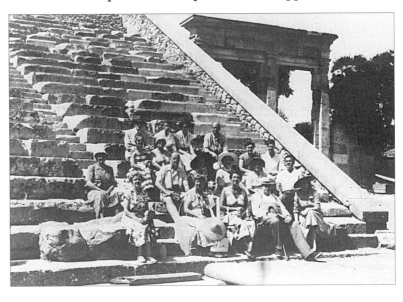

In the theatre at Epidaurus.

with all the conveniences of a small-scale Mediterranean cruise. After visiting the Acropolis and other important sites, they were taken through the Northern Peloponnese, visiting Corinth, Mycaenae and Olympia, then returning via Patras and Delphi where Vaughan Williams was taken to the top of a hill on the back of a pony. They relished the atmosphere of every Classical ruin and enjoyed the unspoilt friendliness of the people, attended a play by Euripides, then travelled to the islands, staying in Crete, visiting Knossos, then sailing to Mykonos where they could observe the sun setting behind Apollo's island across the narrows. After revisiting Athens, they travelled to Venice and the French Loire Valley.

Hardly had they returned than the couple were flying to Ireland where Vaughan Williams delivered the first Arnold Bax Memorial lecture at Cork University, that composer of the 'Celtic Twilight' and unabashed symphonic romantic having died the year before. In his most mischievous and uncompromising manner, Vaughan Williams lectured on the English origins of Irish folk songs – his old friend Bax would have appreciated this, but the audience felt slightly uneasy. Other lectures followed that year and he was honoured at the end by being the first musician to be presented with the Royal Society of Arts Albert Medal, all previous recipients having been artists.

In February 1956 the new symphony was put into rehearsal with the Hallé Orchestra under John Barbirolli in Manchester and Vaughan Williams returned shortly afterwards to conduct the same forces with added soloists and choir in a performance of the *St Matthew Passion*. He was also writing music for a short documentary film about Elizabeth I's England, alternating this with a motet entitled *A Vision of Aeroplanes*. This was a setting of mysterious words by the Old Testament prophet Ezekiel, who had

With Barbirolli and Ursula
at the Free Trade Hall,
Manchester.

122

apparently seen sights similar to flying machines so, once more, Vaughan Williams showed that biblical texts could be treated to a fresh, if controversial interpretation.

When the *Eighth Symphony* was given its first performance at the beginning of May the audience was again treated to something unusual in the Vaughan Williams canon, as well as the typical humorously dismissive programme note by the composer. He called his first movement 'seven variations in search of a theme', although it shows the tight control of a master symphonist. The music continued to intrigue as it progressed through a witty scherzo for wind instruments alone, a slow movement for unaccompanied strings and a Toccata finale which 'commandeers all the available hitting instruments that can make definite notes' including vibraphone and gongs. The whole work seemed to review most areas of Vaughan Williams's musical styles whilst still proving that here was indeed a composer eighty-three years young, as he showed by enjoying himself immensely at the post-performance party. The London première later in the month proved equally successful and Vaughan Williams was so pleased that he dedicated it to the 'Glorious John' who had conducted the first performance, and would also make the first recording. Adrian Boult would also record the symphony later in the year, as he had done with all the others.

No sooner had Vaughan Williams finished this symphony than he began another. He sketched it during the early part of the year and then worked on it to the exclusion of everything else. He took the score with him when he went with Ursula to stay with the Wedgwoods at Leith Hill Place that summer – the last he would spend in his childhood home with his cousin, who died a few

The Lark Ascending, with Frederick Grinke in Gloucester Cathedral.

At Gloucester in 1956, with Herbert Howells, and now hard of hearing.

months later. He also worked on it when they visited their friends the Finzis at Ashmansworth that summer – another final meeting as Gerald would also die that year. It is possible that the passing of these good friends affected the score, which contains much music that is elegiac, bordering at times on the tragic.

Ralph and Ursula attended the Three Choirs Festival in Gloucester in September and heard the *Eighth Symphony* performed together with *Hodie* and *The Lark Ascending*. Shortly afterwards they flew to Majorca. He had had glowing reports of the island from Holst more than forty years before and was not disappointed. They based themselves in the capital, Palma, where they met some old friends and were introduced to the poet Robert Graves, who had made his home in the north-west of the island. They also visited nearby Valdemosa where Chopin had spent one miserable winter in monastery apartments. During their stay, Vaughan Williams made the acquaintance of some local folk dancers, who performed ancient fertility dances for him which he likened to English Morris Dances. It appears that the same 'Moorish' influence was evident in both.

On his return to London, Vaughan Williams, perhaps recalling Holst more closely now he had visited landscapes his friend had loved, set about organising a concert of his neglected music in the Festival Hall as part of a trust he had organised, financed by his own royalties, to help struggling musicians. *Egdon Heath* was played, and many other major, though half-forgotten works, and in doing this, Vaughan Williams made a gallant attempt to keep Holst's memory alive as more than a 'one-work' composer.

Memories of Holst's deep socialist sympathies may have stirred in Vaughan Williams as he watched the Russian Communists crushing democratic reforms in Hungary that year, but his own feelings

In the drawing room at Hanover Terrace.

Travelling in 1957.

were ambiguous. He wrote to a friend that he understood the aims of real communism, but that the Russians had abandoned what he had earlier believed 'used to be a fine creed'. 1956 had been politically eventful in other ways. Britain and France had finally seen their pretensions to imperial world power dashed with their defeat over the Suez crisis, and these realities of diminishing status seemed more in tune with the material tawdriness of post-war Britain than the much-vaunted 'new Elizabethan Age' hailed with such pomp only four years before. To Vaughan Williams, the only valid hope lay in continuing the tradition he, Holst and the other composers of his youth had begun, and he could rest comfortably assured that he had done everything in his own powers to maintain that hope into the future.

Throughout 1957, Vaughan Williams continued to work on the new symphony. He now intended to introduce three saxophones and also a flugelhorn into the orchestra, writing later:

This beautiful and neglected instrument is not usually allowed in the select circles of the orchestra and has been banished to the brass band, where it is allowed to indulge in the bad habit of vibrato to its heart's content. While in the orchestra it will be obliged to sit up and play straight.

Brass band music had always been a passion of his, and his experiments in the Eighth and Ninth symphonies produced some further occasional works that year including his *Variations for Brass Band* written as a test piece for a brass band festival in the Albert Hall and a *Flourish for Glorious John* for the centenary concert of John Barbirolli's Hallé Orchestra.

A trip to Scotland in May to hear the *Sea Symphony* conducted by the Countess of Haddo at Haddo House, with a choir and orchestra mostly consisting of local musicians, made a pleasing break and this was followed by a holiday in Austria. Ralph and Ursula visited Innsbruck and Salzburg, making excursions to the lakes and mountains, and returned via Munich. A performance of *The Poisoned Kiss* with much of the embarrassing dialogue omitted and the libretto largely rewritten by Ursula was given at the Royal Academy of Music shortly afterwards and most agreed that it was now more satisfactory in this updated form. The Prom season that year included performances of the *Sinfonia Antartica* and the *Eighth Symphony* both of which Vaughan Williams attended, but during this period he was forced to enter hospital for an operation.

Apart from a predisposition for bad chills, Vaughan Williams had always enjoyed robust health and was very fit for his age, but he had felt unwell ever since his return from Europe and the operation was the culmination of a whole series of tests which had diagnosed thrombosis. There was a certain amount of anxiety for a man of such advanced years, but the operation proved completely successful and after a period of convalescence he was able to attend his eighty-fifth birthday celebrations at the Festival Hall in October. These included performances of *A Pastoral Symphony*, *On Wenlock*

With Lionel Tertis.

Edge and *Job*. The audience all stood and applauded as he entered, still a little unsteady after his recent illnesses, but with the noble bearing of one of the great classical composers of the past. A private party followed in a London restaurant with tributes including a specially commissioned poem, and hundreds of telegrams and cards arrived at the house from all round the world. A party was given for him in Dorking and another by the Composer's Guild but, amongst all the gifts and tributes, the present he appreciated most was a facsimile copy of Bach's original manuscripts of the *Mass in B minor*.

With the symphony 'finished so far as a composition ever is finished' as he said, Vaughan Williams ended the year writing music to accompany a film of William Blake's pictures, *The Vision of William Blake*, commissioned by the Blake Film Trust to commemorate the bicentenary of his birth. This was a radical departure from his earlier full-blooded orchestral scores, being settings of ten poems from the *Songs of Innocence and Experience* for tenor and oboe alone which he wrote in a white heat of inspiration. This and rehearsals for the two Bach Passions in Dorking filled the winter, together with preparations for the first performance of the new symphony, to be given by Malcolm Sargent and the Royal Philharmonic Orchestra in the Festival Hall.

Vaughan Williams conducted the two Bach Passions at the Leith

Rehearsing for the world premiere of the 9th Symphony in St Pancras Town Hall, 1958.

Hill Festival in March with all his usual authority and had a private recording made of the *St Matthew Passion* which gives valuable insights into his 'unauthentic' but deeply-felt interpretation of the work. 'I think our performance of the Passion last night was the best we have done,' he wrote next day. He attended the two rehearsal performances of the new *Symphony No. 9 in E minor* in St Pancras Town Hall, London and once more appeared to a standing ovation in the Ceremonial Box for the première in early April 1958, a public performance relayed live by BBC radio . The symphony was noble and magisterial in outline, although Vaughan Williams had once more provided a flippant programme note in which he stated amongst other things that the composer slips in a repeat of a theme, having 'forgotten' to do so in the right place and that the saxophones behave in the scherzo 'like demented cats'. The flugelhorn worked its unexpected magic and the music made a deep impression on an enthusiastic audience, although some critics were baffled, finding reworkings of earlier music in the score. There is a sense that Vaughan Williams was reviewing his whole career as a composer in the symphony, but it is very largely 'recollected in tranquillity', a masterful summing up by one of the finest symphonists of the twentieth century.

After the tensions of the previous two months, Ralph and Ursula set off for their annual holiday. They flew to Naples, saw Herculaneum and the coastal towns nearby and travelled to Ischia where William Walton and his wife lent them their own house. Although it rained for much of the early part of their stay, fine weather returned and they were able to visit Capri. It was too commercialised for their taste, but they enjoyed the remainder of their break and, on returning to London, Vaughan Williams was sufficiently energetic to travel to Nottingham University and receive another honorary Doctorate of Music. This was followed by a tour round Lincolnshire in June

127

With John Barbirolli and the Hallé Orchestra.

and a visit to the Cheltenham Festival in July to hear *A London Symphony* performed by John Barbirolli and the Hallé Orchestra. After the performance the conductor and his wife entertained Ralph and Ursula for dinner at a nearby hotel. Barbirolli recalled:

It was a beautiful evening and the Malvern Hills could be seen clearly ... We stayed at the supper table until after 2 am, the old man in wonderful form, telling story after story, and even if he did nod off for a moment or two occasionally he seemed to awake with better and even funnier tales.

There was a performance of the *Ninth Symphony* at the Proms which Ralph and Ursula attended, and plans were made to record it at the end of August with Adrian Boult conducting. They were also able to attend a revival of *Sir John in Love* staged by the new Opera Company before taking another English break, travelling to the West Country where they visited Salisbury and explored Thomas Hardy's 'Wessex' at its magnificently rural best. When they returned to London, Vaughan Williams continued to work on an opera he and Ursula had concocted together and a nativity play for which he had been asked to compose and arrange music, but he was not to finish these. On 26th August 1958 he had intended

128

to join Adrian Boult and the London Philharmonic Orchestra for the recording of the *Ninth Symphony* but instead Adrian Boult was left alone to preface the recording with these words:

We had hoped that our beloved friend Ralph Vaughan Williams would have been with us in the studio while we were recording this symphony but his death took place seven hours before we began our work on it.

He had passed away peacefully in his sleep and, when John Barbirolli arrived at Hanover Terrace that morning to pay his respects, he saw his 'noble head … like a magnificent effigy of some noble medieval Prelate'. At the same moment, Adrian Boult lifted his baton to conduct Vaughan Williams's last symphony. It was a moving and tragic performance – a fitting tribute to one of the greatest and kindest composers England had produced.

Epilogue

On 19 September 1958, the funeral service for Ralph Vaughan Williams took place in Westminster Abbey. Amongst the music he had requested there was a seventeenth-century funeral motet, his own motet *O Taste and See*, his magnificent setting of *The Old Hundredth* complete with trumpets and the 'Pavane for the Sons of the Morning' from *Job*. The bronze casket containing his ashes was taken in procession to the Musician's Corner in the north aisle whilst the congregation sang the hymn *Come Down O Love Divine* to his own setting *Down Ampney*. Arthur Bliss, the Master of the Queen's Musick, spoke the tribute:

Vaughan Williams grew in stature as the years went by like some magnificent tree. At the end, his mind was full of music. He was always an explorer, a searcher. He was a great man as we judge great men and it is wholly fitting that he should be laid to rest in the Abbey beside Purcell and Handel.

Born in the Victorian Age and surviving through some of the worst as well as some of the most exciting changes in the twentieth century, Vaughan Williams's achievement was that he had built an enduring legacy based on the music of ordinary people, creating works in every form that rivalled the most contemporary of composers. Yet he had never lost the common touch and, despite the tragedies and frustrations that attend every human being, he had lived to the full. As George Trevelyan had written to him five years before, 'We have had fortunate lives in a very unfortunate age.'

Bibliography

Sources used in preparation of text

Heirs and Rebels – Letters and Occasional Writings by Ralph Vaughan Williams and Gustav Holst – ed. Ursula Vaughan Williams and Imogen Holst (OUP, 1959)
National Music and Other Essays by Ralph Vaughan Williams (OUP, 1969)
R.V.W. a Biography of Ralph Vaughan Williams by Ursula Vaughan Williams (OUP, 1964)
The Works of Ralph Vaughan Williams by Michael Kennedy (OUP, 1964) [*passim*]
Ralph Vaughan Williams – a pictorial biography by John E. Lunn & Ursula Vaughan Williams (OUP, 1971)

Other suggested reading

Vaughan Williams (The Master Musician Series) by James Day (J.M. Dent & Sons Ltd, 1961, rev. 1975)

Vaughan Williams: Compact Disc Recordings

Concertos for Oboe, Violin, Tuba, Piano;
also *The Lark Ascending, Two Hymn Tune
Preludes, Toward the Unknown Region,
Concerto Grosso, Partita for Double String
Orchestra*
    David Theodore, Kenneth Sillito,
    Patrick Harrild, Michael Davis,
    Howard Shelley/LSO/LSO Chorus/
    Bryden Thomson
    Chandos CHAN 9262/3

Piano Concerto; also Delius: Piano Concerto and Finzi: *Eclogue*
    Piers Lane/RLPO/
    Vernon Handley
    EMI CD-EMX 2239

English Folk Songs Suite, Fantasia on
Greensleeves, *In the Fen Country, The Lark
Ascending, Norfolk Rhapsody No.1, Serenade
to Music*
    16 soloists/Hugh Bean/LPO, LSO
    or New Philh Orch/
    Sir Adrian Boult
    EMI CDM7 64022-2

*The Wasps: Overture, Fantasia on a Theme
by Thomas Tallis, Five Variants of Dives
and Lazarus, In the Fen Country, Norfolk
Rhapsody No. 1, Variations for Orchestra*
(orch. Gordon Jacob)
    ASMF, Neville Marriner
    Ph. 442 427-2

*Fantasia on Greensleeves, Fantasia on a
Theme by Thomas Tallis; also Elgar: Intro-
duction and Allegro for Strings, Serenade for
Strings, Elegy, Sospiri*
    Sinfonia of London/Allegri String
    Quartet/Sir John Barbirolli
    EMI CDC7 47537-2

*Job (A Masque for Dancing), Variations for
Orchestra* (orch. Gordon Jacob)
    Bournemouth SO/Richard Hickox
    EMI CDC7 54421-2

Symphonies 1 – 9; also *Flos Campi, Serenade
to Music* (choral version)
    Christopher Balmer (viola)/
    Soloists/Liverpool Philharmonic
    Choir/RLPO/Vernon Handley
    EMI CD-BOXVW 1 (6)
    (also available separately)

Symphony No. 1 (*A Sea Symphony*)
    Felicity Lott/Jonathan Summers/
    London Philharmonic Choir/
    LPO/Bernard Haitink
    EMI CDC7 49911-2

Symphony No. 2 (*A London Symphony*);
also *Fantasia on a Theme by Thomas Tallis*
    LPO/Sir Adrian Boult
    EMI CDM7 64017-2

Symphony No. 2 (*A London Symphony*)
(1920 version); also Walton: Violin Concerto
(first recording, with Jascha Heifetz), etc.
    Cincinnati SO/Eugene Goossens
    Biddulph WHL 016

Symphony No. 3 (*A Pastoral Symphony*);
also Symphony No.4
    Heather Harper/LSO/André Previn
    RCA GD 90503 [60583-2-RG]

Symphony No.4; also Symphony No. 5
    (No.4) BBC SO/Composer;
    (No.5) Hallé Orch/John Barbirolli
    Dutton Lab. CDAX 8011

Symphony No.5; also *The Lark Ascending,
Norfolk Rhapsody No. 1*
    Sarah Chang/LPO/Bernard Haitink
    EMI CDC5 55487-2

Symphony No. 6; also *The Lark Ascending,
Fantasia on a Theme by Thomas Tallis*
    BBC SO/Andrew Davis;
    also Tasmin Little (violin)
    Teldec/Warner 9031 73127-2

Symphony No. 6 (with speech by the Composer); also Symphony No. 4
    LPO/Sir Adrian Boult
    Belart mono 461/117 2/10

Symphony No. 7 (*Sinfonia Antartica*)
    Sheila Armstrong/
    London Philharmonic Chorus/
    LPO/Bernard Haitink
    EMI CDC7 47516-2

Symphony No. 8; also Symphony No. 9,
Flourish for Glorious John
    Philharmonia Orch/
    Leonard Slatkin
    RCA 09026 61196-2

Symphony No. 8; also Symphony No. 2 (*A London Symphony*)
    Hallé Orch/Sir John Barbirolli
    EMI CDM7 64197-2

Symphony No. 9; also Arnold: Symphony No. 3
    LPO, Sir Adrian Boult
    Everest EVC 9001

Phantasy Quintet, String Quartet No. 2, Six Studies in English Folk-Song, Violin Sonata in A
    Music Group of London/
    Eileen Croxford/
    David Parkhouse/Hugh Bean
    EMI CDM5 65100-2

Toward the Unknown Region, Dona Nobis Pacem, Four Hymns, Lord, thou hast been our refuge (Psalm 90), *O clap your hands* (Psalm 47)
    Judith Howarth/John Mark Ainsley/
    Thomas Allen/Corydon Singers
    & Orch/Matthew Best
    Hyperion CDA 66655

Sancta Civitas, Dona Nobis Pacem
    Yvonne Kenny, Philip Langridge,
    Bryn Terfel, St Paul's Cathedral
    Choristers/London Symphony Chorus
    and Orch/Richard Hickox
    EMI CDC 7 54788-2

Epithalamion, Merciless Beauty, Riders to the Sea
    Stephen Roberts/Howard Shelley/
    Bach Choir/LPO/Willcocks;
    Philip Langridge/Endellion Quartet;
    Norma Burrowes/Margaret Price/
    Helen Watts/Benjamin Luxon/
    Ambrosian Singers/Orch Nova of
    London/Meredith Davies
    EMI CDM7 64730-2

Folk Song Arrangements; also works by other composers
    London Madrigal Singers/
    Christopher Bishop
    EMI CMS5 65123-2

On Wenlock Edge, Ten Blake Songs, Four Hymns, Merciless Beauty, The New Ghost, The Water Mill
    Ian Partridge/Janet Craxton/
    Jennifer Partridge/
    Music Group of London
    EMI CDM5 65589-2

The Pilgrim's Progress (incidental music, edited Christopher Palmer)
    Sir John Gielgud/Richard Pasco/
    Ursula Howells/Corydon Singers/
    City of London Sinfonia/
    Matthew Best
    Hyperion CDA 66511

The Pilgrim's Progress
    Richard Whitehouse, Wyn Griffiths
    & soloists, Choir and Orch of
    Royal N Coll of Music/
    Igor Kennaway
    RNCM PP1/2
    (available from the Royal Northern
    College of Music, Manchester)

Hugh the Drover
    Bonaventura Bottone/
    Rebecca Evans/Sarah Walker/
    Richard Van Allan/Alan Opie/
    Corydon Singers & Orch/
    Matthew Best
    Hyperion CDSA 66901/2

Film music: *Coastal Command* (Suite), *England of Elizabeth, 49th Parallel* (Prelude), *Story of a Flemish Farm* (Suite)
    RTE Concert Orch/Andrew Penny
    Marco Polo 8.223665

Index

135

136

137

141

142